Three

Plastic

Rooms

Three Plastic Rooms

A novel

Petra Hůlová

Translated from the Czech by
Alex Zucker

Jantar Publishing
London 2017

First published in London, Great Britain in 2017 by
Jantar Publishing Ltd
www.jantarpublishing.com

Czech edition first published by nakladatelství Torst, Prague, in 2006 as
Umělohmotný třípokoj

Petra Hůlová
Three Plastic Rooms
All rights reserved

Original text © Petra Hůlová
English translation copyright © 2017 Alex Zucker
Cover and book design by Jack Coling

A CIP catalogue record for this book is available from the British Library.
ISBN 978-0-9933773-9-6

Printed and bound in the Czech Republic by EUROPRINT a.s.

This book has been selected to receive financial assistance from
English PEN's "PEN Translates" programme.

  Supported using public funding by
ARTS COUNCIL
ENGLAND

This translation was made possible by a grant from the Ministry of Culture of the Czech Republic.

 MINISTRY OF CULTURE
CZECH REPUBLIC

Contents

Introduction
Three Plastic Rooms of One's Own

Petra Hůlová's writing career began in Mongolia. During a year as an exchange student there she began writing what would eventually become her first novel, a first-person narrative about three generations of women in a Mongolian family. Published in 2002, that novel has since appeared in English translation as *All This Belongs to Me* (trans. Alex Zucker [Evanston, IL: Northwestern University Press, 2009]). The novel made its 23-year-old author an immediate sensation, winning some of the most prestigious Czech literary prizes and appearing in translation in several languages within the next few years. The novel's success abroad is more significant than might first

appear, since it broke a long-dominant trend—most marked in the English-language literary market—that authors from what was once called 'the Other Europe' must represent and reflect upon their own society and politics: Czech novels were to have Czech characters, not Mongolian. Hůlová stood at the beginning of a fresh trend within Czech literature at the beginning of the 21st century to explore the world rather than brood about home. Since then she has published seven further novels, some still in this cosmopolitan vein (set in Siberia or New York City) and others with distinctly Czech settings or themes (exploring perceptions of the collapse of communism in Czechoslovakia, or the experiences of a Ukrainian 'guest-worker' in the present-day Czech Republic). The present novel, which appeared in 2006, lies somewhere in between, since it focuses on the world's oldest profession—a universal theme. While this novel also won a major Czech literary prize, it evoked controversy due to its explicit, at times brutal exploration of the ambivalent forces of sexuality. It is perhaps reassuring to know that in the 21st century a novel about sex can still make us uncomfortable.

One major source of discomfort is that the reader is hard pressed to know what to make of the narrator, a prostitute fixated on the incipient signs of ageing in her body. One has the distinct sense that the narrator has confronted a difficult life with strength and resilience, but she is by no means a 'pure-hearted prostitute' in the Dostoyevskian mould. Moral ambiguity predominates. The narrator is alternately sym-

pathetic and alienating: At times she wins our admiration for her merciless insight into social hypocrisy and at times provokes revulsion through her own indulgent complicity. Simultaneously, the vulgarity of her language would make a seasoned sailor blush, yet gradually mesmerizes the reader. One of the major achievements of the novel is that these moral and linguistic ambiguities manage to be simultaneously horrifying and humorous.

How should one think about such ambiguities? Is the novel making light of these serious topics, or perhaps hiding behind some breezy relativism? By no means. The philosopher and literary critic Walter Benjamin wrote, in Marxist terms, about the figure of the prostitute as a human being forced into the role of a commodity. The exploitative aspect of such role is obvious enough: Human characteristics, the uniqueness of the individual, are erased under the objectifying gaze of the customer, and are replaced by a price tag and timer-clock. The prostitute, in other words, is a human being transfigured into an object for sale, or at least for rent. But Benjamin's conception opens another side to this process, a more analytical angle, if you will: The prostitute represents a commodity endowed with human agency. From this perspective the prostitute can acquire, and therefore perhaps communicate, critical insight into the darker workings of consumer society. Such insight carries particular weight, arising as it does from the prostitute's position as a cog, willing or more likely unwilling, in the social and sexual machinery.

The narrator of *Three Plastic Rooms* embodies both sides of this dynamic. She is at times an exploited commodity (and exploiter of other commodities), and at other times our informer, our 'agent in the field', reporting on how things really work at ground level in a thoroughly commodified environment. Her complete submersion in the system which exploits her is revealed through her chosen form of escape: At regular intervals she locks the doors of her flat—which she proudly calls her 'fuckshop'—and goes to the mall for an espresso and a shopping spree. These escapes clearly remain within the realm of commodity consumption, an affinity underlined by her language. Her cash flow, as she points out, is generated directly by her customers' ejaculations, and her jaunts outside of her three plastic rooms take place under the sign of her plastic credit card. Further, the narrator periodically launches into jeremiads against the 'e-world' of mobile phones, webpages, video-screens, and computerized toys, which replace real human contact with digital interactions. But technology (Internet, mobile phones) is also a crucial instrument of her business. She also exercises her imagination by thinking up ideas for television documentaries about overlooked yet fundamental mysteries of contemporary life, such as: Whether women in menopause who have to carry multiple extra blouses to change into when they sweat too much will firm up their figures by carrying the large pocketbooks required for those blouses; or how older, retired women who eat nothing but chicken broth for a week in order to afford birthday gifts for

their grandchildren nevertheless manage to remain fat; or why in poverty-stricken countries people burn wood to heat water when that wood contains more calories than the water—and similar questions we have all asked ourselves. The world of media consumption, inseparable from the e-world she vilifies, is thus one in which she has an obsessive interest and displays a remarkable degree of comfort and mastery.

At other times, however, the narrator forces shocked recognition of truths that are uncomfortable indeed. The most disturbing such moment comes during her discussion of paedophiles. This is one of the few topics about which the narrator appears to have a clear moral compass: 'There is no excuse in this world [for them], and if there is a hell, then fwoop, down they all go'. She mocks the idea that psychological analysis might reveal such people to be victims (perhaps themselves once targets of childhood abuse) or help to understand and thereby relativize their actions. None the less, she takes the reader on her own thought experiment in a different form of understanding. She challenges the reader to enter the paedophile's head and *truly* understand his motivations and sensations. And she warns: beware—beware. There follows an extended description of a paedophile's molestation presented not with critical distance, not through the filter of moral or basic human outrage, but with extraordinarily disturbing understanding, even empathy: the empathy of someone for whom the amorality or violence of sexuality is intimately familiar. When her description ends, her moral stance is as

clear as before: Understanding has not altered judgment. But the narrator's thought experiment, based on her own intense familiarity with the raw power of these ominous, chthonic forces, has revealed that they will not be dispelled by mere expressions of moral indignation. Here lies the darkness at the heart of this novel.

While the narrator pursues a profession that is rarely associated with linguistic creativity, her language is in fact strikingly inventive. Two terms stand out: *sticker-inner* and *hammer*. These are the narrator's terms for female and male sexual organs and, unsurprisingly, they play an important role in the novel. But their significance goes beyond the fact that they are the tools of the narrator's trade. In fact, *sticker-inner* and *hammer* evolve into two of the novel's main characters. As readers we become familiar with their moods, habits and whims. They pout, get angry, get bored. They work hard, they become tired. They flap about like fish in the mud, or they hop to attention. Not mere nouns, they transform into verbs and other grammatical forms, giving rise to surprising formulations. In short, they assert their independence. At one point the narrator teasingly scolds her sticker-inner, which has mischievously left embarrassing stains at an inconvenient moment. At another point she speaks of her head as 'a stand-alone unit, since my head isn't me, just like my sticker-inner isn't, and if I'm something half-and-half, created from their union, then I don't know what that is'. The narrator's subjectivity appears to be no more than the sum of her body parts,

which emerge as independent agents. In Czech, not only are nouns gendered (as in Spanish or German) but the gender of nouns is reflected in verb forms as well. And—it had to be!—'sticker-inner' (*zandavák* in Czech) is a masculine noun and 'hammer' (*rašple*, in Czech literally a rasp or file) is a feminine noun. So there are many contorted interactions between these two nouns where their grammatical and biological genders work at cross purposes.

These word-characters are one of the means by which the novel transforms what on one level is the sheer, banal repetition of sexually explicit situations into extraordinary linguistic inventiveness. But before one waxes too wistful about the excellent adventures of *sticker-inner* and *hammer* it is important to note another ambiguity. At times this fecund linguistic inventiveness itself devolves into a flat, suffocating environment—a plastic landscape of bright though artificial colour. These words *do* in fact perform the same dance over and over. This is, therefore, a further linguistic counterpart to the moral ambiguities discussed above. *Sticker-inner* and *hammer* are simultaneously vehicles for creative escape and bricks in the plastic prison in which the narrator is locked. For these reasons the laughter this novel provokes—and, despite the disturbing subject, reading it is often a giddy pleasure—is always accompanied by an uncomfortable glance out the window.

The linguistic play has a further effect: The narrator, despite her foibles, has a degree of charm. For all her moral failings, we cannot denigrate her entirely—not least because she is

responding to the unsavoury life in which she is trapped with strength and a sort of creativity. The question thus arises: Is this a feminist novel? Not in any obvious sense that would be reducible to a specific message or argument. The narrator hardly comes off as the stoic victim of a sexist society. She seems too comfortable with her lot for such an interpretation, and indeed some of her own views betray more than a whiff of misogyny. Yet the English-language reader is likely to be reminded of what is probably the most famous reflection on gender inequality in literary production. Our narrator has her own source of modest yet sufficient income, and she does have a room of her own—in fact, she has three. But these rooms have not brought meaningful freedom; they are just a fuckshop. So the narrator's dilemma of entrapment has evolved from that described by Virginia Woolf in *A Room of One's Own*. If *Three Plastic Rooms* provides any focal symbol of this contemporary dilemma, it is less the plastic rooms themselves and more the narrator's beloved object in those rooms: her pet bird, moulded from plastic as if it were a sex toy and imported from China. That plastic bird is colourful, attractive, and offers the semblance of companionship, but will never fly and never sing.

Peter Zusi
Highgate
July 2017

x

TV Episode One:
Women With Handbags

I wonder if anyone ever gives her a grinding down to the bone? That one there, who doesn't take care of herself and stuffs her face with whatever she feels like. I wonder if her slit too is like a peephole into a lobby with a blown-out lightbulb, a long dark narrow hallway that can turn supple and slicken, and tighten and choke like elastic on a pair of panties? I wonder whether hers does that too? I wonder if she knows how to strangle a snake until it turns red, to take hold of it by the throat and give it a proper yanking? Because if she did, she would have no reason to take care of herself anymore, and wouldn't have to worry that her makeup was expired, crusty, and peeling

off in strips like the damp plaster of the building where she sits out every day.

I see her when I walk past. Out there on the corner, where the overhang makes for a cozy feel in spite of the piss that rains against the wall every night from the men who think that nobody can see them in the dark and that no one will come walking by at such a late hour. Her hair is short and her fat face is covered in red spots, but they aren't pimples. She just scrubs her face too hard before she goes out. I don't think it helps.

I wonder if any man has ever turned to look at her out of sheer eagerness, and decided to choose her because she has something to give? Probably not, or she wouldn't be sitting there so downcast every morning, looking like she was waiting to be rescued.

Some women hardly take care of themselves at all. They get fat and think no one will notice as long as they dress in loose-fitting clothes. I suppose that no one has ever told them high heels aren't for comfort, you wear them to make your legs look slim. Women like that don't walk the streets, much less strut them. They plod along the sidewalk like they were wading through leafsludge in a neglected city park, and they may think that it's all the same, but it's not.

Don't stink and watch your weight. Those are the most important resolutions I know of. Every morning I plop myself down in front of the mirror and stare into my face, just in case

it might finally tell me something I don't know. It stares right back, as if expecting the same from me. We'll never settle anything doing it like that, but still, every morning I try just the same. Maybe one day it will give in. Sometimes it looks like a wisp of myself. Smirking at me with the innocent grin of a bird. Then again, other times it looks like it was slapped together from rags, like a hastily stitched soccer ball, and it's asking for a kick, too, and all this in the time it takes us to reach a lasting agreement. Meanwhile the stool has imprinted a square into my rear and I can feel parts of my own edges, the ones that don't hold together too well, overflowing the stool's edges, even though I'm not overweight. It's always lovely to have your day get off to a cheerful start.

If I had a courtyard, I would sweep it from corner to corner using a birch broom I bound together myself, and every time I did my chores, I would feel like one of those women at the country fairs who dress in traditional folk costume. Not like in the room where I wake, occasionally with a man at my side, surrounded by molded plastic. Including my little yellow molded-plastic bird, though its cage is metal, just like a real bird's. I take great joy in the ingenuity of human invention. Everybody's little yellow plastic bird is the same, pumped out of a machine in the far reaches of China, and so even if it was produced by child labor it still bears a whiff of the distant lands from whence it came, no matter that it flew on the wings of a Boeing.

At least it will never abandon me for warmer climes in Africa. I already get sad every fall as it is, when the birds

begin to disappear. They roost even though no one forces them to, which takes some real self-discipline, so I wave at them from the street, and at least in that small way I share in their concerns. Apart from that, it doesn't mean much in my life, I'm not the depressive type. Never have been. Some might say disorderly house, but I call it a human nest, filled with warmth and cozy corners hiding all kinds of surprises. Including the used tissues that fall behind the bed when I squirm too much at night. I slip them under my pillow after I blow my nose, and I'm not sure if they have retractable legs, or maybe more like cat's claws in tiny little sheaths, but somehow or other they get down there, and within a few weeks they're nice and hard. Then later, when I try to smooth them out, they crackle like the radio, or the way the radio would crackle if it weren't e-.

The e-world plagues me, it makes me feel I'm not fast enough, even if I am still young and hairless and need warmth and caressing to blossom like the flower that every woman is, and nowadays men are flowers too and also need to be cared for. So much work goes into caring, and the labor force for it is lacking, and that's why it's so important for our labor market to be open to outsiders, who aren't yet exhausted by the ups and downs of daily life, though it's true they don't take such good care of their looks, which puts them at a bit of a disadvantage on our streets. But flaws are part of the e-world too, since otherwise there would be nothing to improve upon, and large-scale industry would wilt like a lily.

The cheap manpower is what I like best, when they stand in the street, sunning themselves, leaning on their shovels, sweat beading on their dark, firm arms. I'm sure they could use a back massage, but they won't come out and say so. Instead they just stand there puffing away, hiding inside a cloud of tobacco smoke, though they could easily hold their own in any local bodybuilding contest. And of course, if you're a bodybuilder, massages come with the territory. Muscles need to be kneaded in order to remain supple yet still be pumped enough for the audience in the back rows. But I just walk right past those men with the shovels, sunken in manholes up to their waists, just as I do past the fat woman with the short hair on the corner, my brain just quietly kneading the little marble of my thoughts.

Years from now, when my periods stop, and I sweat like a dog even in winter, I'll have to trade in my purse for a proper handbag to make sure that I have enough room for a backup supply of blouses. I can carry the weight, and it might help keep my body firm, assuming that anyone still cares about it by that point.

These are the kinds of mysteries that deserve a special TV series all their own. A series illuminating the little mysteries of life that we otherwise dismiss. Are we all really just stationmasters waving our signal discs up and down, traffic police directing motorists in a traffic jam? Let them go right on waving their arms along with the rest of the idiots while I fill the gap in the market, since we don't have an educational

series like that yet. The whole thing's my idea, I came up with it just now, and I promise, I'll be thinking about it the whole time, from here on in. You'll see how well suited to teamwork I am. I've got ten people I can count on every finger, at least on some days of the week.

In fact, dump out any one of the drawers in my desk and you'll have material lined up like beads on a string. Every scuffed and used little item in there is a story, and a hairpin with a year-and-a-half-old fistful of hair could be two, even four, because the human body reeks of intrigue from a hundred miles away, and a story is one long thread of problems, everyone would get bored otherwise. I enjoy stories of broken hearts too, even if I don't know the people, they're made-up, so they aren't instructive, so there's actually no reason to care. Still, the only time I find myself squeezing one of my hands with the other is while watching an e-story. I either check them out of the library or buy them from the store, even if I rarely bother to watch them more than once. Afterwards, I sleep like a baby, like I'm in a rowboat floating downstream, intrepidly conquering all the rapids in its path, only to wake up again in the morning back in a room full of molded plastic, which only my little yellow birdie from China can rightfully claim as his, but still it managed to find its way in here somehow, that's just how it works with households. I open my eyes and see my purchases all around me. Meanwhile, if I were still asleep, I would be grinning like a newborn, and who would ever think an infant like that would head out to the shopping

mall with a credit card to brighten his day? Warm milk and mama's crooning are all a little baby needs. Nighty-night, I tell myself when I can't get to sleep, and imagine myself not knowing how to talk or walk, since slumber can't help but take pity on a helpless little bundle of joy, all greased up with nighttime cream.

Sometimes I also put on a warm little woolen cap to keep everything nice and tight on my head, so my hair won't get tousled and disturb my sleep, which my head deserves the same as all the rest of my extremities, and especially my sticker-inner, so tired out from the banging the hammers give it, I'm afraid he'll never open wide like an umbrella again.

Usually, when it's tired, my sticker-inner just sits blowing bubbles like a little fish stuck in the mud at the bottom of a nearly drained pond, although with somewhat less strenuousness, it isn't as if his life is at stake. All he wants is a few hours of uninterrupted quiet, nothing that he would have to reimburse me for, and besides he doesn't even have hands and I'm the one who takes the cash. Still, there are times when the way he whines you would think his life actually sort of was at stake. All those deep breaths in and out, what is that? Maybe just trapped air and he's trying to puff it all out now? But there can't be that much, can there? Maybe he's gotten spoiled from too much attention and now he's just grumbling into his beard? If I squeeze my knees all the way together, he usually stops. Maybe he's overlubricated and doesn't like the feeling that he can't find his way around.

I usually devote attention to my sticker-inner every day before I go to sleep. Sometimes I give him a little extra, but if I touch him when he doesn't want to, he breaks out in goose-bumps and hisses like an angry tomcat protecting his den, and I would have to be a half-wit not to understand. So then I tell him, "Sorry, I didn't realize," but I did, it's just that I didn't feel like going to sleep and I thought he could take a little bit more, since if he had been totally fucky-fucked out I would have fallen flat on my face, like a soldier hit by a bullet, and plunging straight to sleep like that is even better than drifting there in a rowboat after an e-film.

When it's a deep sleep, it doesn't wrap around my head like a python cable, but sneaks up on me out of nowhere and bops me on the skull, so even if morning comes in with a roar, at least it's much more graceful. Physically fit, with menthol-fresh breath from the moment I awake, my thighs practically wrapping themselves in the blue-and-black spandex leggings I wear on my pre-breakfast runs.

Morning, teardrop-shaped and aerodynamically stream-lined like the latest hip-chic cycling helmet, shoots me out onto the street straight as a dart and right on target. My sneakers race along the riverside all by themselves and my sticker-inner keeps to himself, not even complaining when he bleeds, just contentedly bouncing along, at most giving a little tickle to let me know that he's in good spirits today.

Most of the time, however, things aren't so idyllic that all my parts run like clockwork without any backtalk. When it's

quick and easy, that's always cause for celebration, but more often we fight and wrestle, elbows fly, and I spend my time searching for socks and stray brassieres.

Some day I'd like to do research on the independent motion of objects. The bras that go missing after a wild gentleman caller's visit, the hankies with the little legs that jump off the bed and hide underneath. Then I would take my diploma and fly off to some exotic place with those nasty birds that roost on the balustrade by the river in September. Whenever I go running past them in the morning, they get spooked and fly up in the air like a gunshot went off, spraying microbes and pathogenic germs everywhere.

That means I have to take a bath before and after. Before, all over, and afterwards too, if I have time.

You could figure out much faster how long it takes to get from one end of the city to the other if time didn't twist and turn and change speed. The thing is, that kind of thinking shouldn't even be allowed, because the moment I get lost in thought, time takes off at full gallop, but as soon as I stop, time stands still with me, even if I urge it on and give it a little nudge by trying to think of something that would distract me and make it confused.

I imagine what my life would be like in a church, or sitting by the entrance to the public toilets with a coin dish on a little table, wearing a nylon smock.

It has to be something extreme, so my fantasy can let loose, like my nose when I have a cold in my room of molded plastic,

or an elevator with its line cut, plunging down the shaft in an action film, although my fantasy is really more the flighty type. It calls a shovel a shovel, it's winged and without borders, like aid to people in disasters from people who are kind. I'd also like to contribute somehow, so there would be more goodness in the world and we wouldn't always have to go looking for it with a safety pin, although gloomy outlooks like that don't exactly help spread it either. It might help to use different words. Instead of "If you wish to be good, first believe you are bad," maybe we should say, "If you wish to be good, first believe you are sad." Who knows? Taking a look at our manner of speaking for a start might not be as trivial as it seems when you consider that a tongue can't lend a hand, since it hasn't got one, or write a travelogue to show how things work in other parts of the world, since people are too lazy to go and see for themselves, and besides not being able to write or travel, a tongue is also soft, and it may be a muscle but, like a client, it's still delicate, vulnerable and at the service of somebody's head, and occasionally of chewing gum too.

Still, I couldn't do my job without it, and my coworker shouldn't be slandered for no reason other than the fact that it's convenient. People who treat those nearest to them as strangers and deny their significance will always pay for it in the end, and anyone who has the good fortune to know this lesson already would be foolish to act like he didn't. To give you an example, the trunk of an elephant on the Indian sub-continent can lift the trunk of a freshly felled tree like it was a

piece of cake, and can probably also take care of the splinters. Even in the e-age, then, elephants can be of great help to man, although manual labor may be sexy, no one uses it that I know of, but nowadays, who even knows that an elephant's tongue isn't called a trunk?

Anyway, knowledge like that is of no use when it comes to everyday errands, and if everything I learned in school were to fall behind the bed along with my dirty handkerchiefs, it wouldn't matter one bit. But meanwhile all those bits of knowledge are stored away in one of my cerebral lobes, stacked one on top of the other like food in the fridge, and whenever I want to draw on it, I have to take an axe to them, they're frozen to the bone in there, at least they won't go bad. If old knowledge stank too, pretty soon we would all be smoked in the stench, and it's bad enough as is, what with all the odors singing forth from our armpits and our crotches. It's one of those songs that goes on and on, and the chorus repeats on the tram every summer, when people with shaggy armpits climb on in their sleeveless dresses and shirts. In smaller towns, with awareness campaigns that teach clean ears and nails, they also bow and doff their hats. And rightly so. Could we be e- too? Oh no, not us. It's just the people who sing that song, begging for others' attention.

Probably no one would have noticed me either, if it hadn't been for that stain that my sticker-inner dribbled onto the back of my dress again this month, this time unexpectedly. Not to make it out to be worse than it was, it wasn't so much that

11

it smelled bad as that people could see it. "Miss," was all the man said, as if I were restocking shelves and he couldn't read the price tag on his package of condoms, but at the same time he was curious to see if I would blush. I didn't look anything like a temp worker, though. I didn't have a name tag that said Jarmila or Monika, or one of those harried-looking photos that they add to it once you've been there a while. That was what threw me about his "Miss." We weren't in a supermarket or a dance class, we were on a tram headed for Červený Vrch, aka Red Heights, and, of course, it goes without saying, the stain on my dress was red too. Oh, sticker-inner, sticker-inner. Ever the magician. Conjuring up a surprise for me not even two hours after I showered. The man, on the other hand, had done a good deed, which was also thanks to the sticker-inner's inability to talk, so it couldn't tell me about the stain, which is why the man had to tell me. Still, the sticker-inner knew exactly what he was doing. Even after I got off and started walking, he was still puffing away with satisfaction at having gotten rid of all that excess mucus yet again. All that red algae that grows in there, and not one bit was left.

Besides the TV mystery series, whose first episode would among other things try to assess how large a handbag filled with spare blouses a woman ought to carry if she's just entered menopause and, like me, is a Virgo, I dream of having a tiny mower to trim the red algae of my ceaselessly growing mucus, since I would use that before I ever bought a handbag as big as the one that my series would recommend to me.

The mower would be red, with a shiny hood, the size of a ladybug, and operate by remote control. My sticker-inner could call it whatever he wanted, and knowing him it would be something funny, he's a real comedian. Then I could just peel back the curtains, like I do every time a hammer comes rushing in, and call in that the mower was on its way, so the sticker-inner could put himself shipshape in two meaty ripples, smack his lips, and have nothing left to do but wait like a gentleman in tweed for the plumber to come calling, though it must be said the sticker-inner usually isn't that strait-laced. Besides, a tweed coat would be too classy for the occasion, and a red algae mower is much less a plumber than it is a gardener's assistant, who are known for their sexual appetite, so a sticker-inner happens to be a convenient place of employment.

Of course that doesn't mean the sticker-inner always has an appetite. In fact he practically has none left at all, and usually has to be convinced like some kind of prima donna, as if he were somebody special, but the only thing unique about him is he's mine, and he belongs to me, even if, like my men, he sometimes doesn't think so.

I like to leave them in there, for that atmosphere of lust that gets them ruffled up. Because once a woman is no longer her sticker-inner's master and the hammer is in charge, there's no need to speak another word and titillation comes to you, slinking on all fours. No longer peeking in through the keyhole, she's dropped her robe and has nothing on beneath except a slip, and her thighs are just the right plumpness and she's

every bit as tight as the hammer dreamed she'd be. Then she whispers into the silence, "Take that filthy cock of yours and plow me good and hard," and by this point the gentlemen's hammer is getting a nice airing out and there are little milky droplets forming on the tip. This is an art unto itself, since it's all in the nuances, just a hair away from ordinary dirty talk, which works best on the red-blooded, simpleminded hammers, but has a less than salutary effect on the shy ones, who picture something a bit more on the delicate side, so you always have to weigh these things carefully in advance.

A little bit of stress, though, works on all of them. You just have to be careful not to overdo it, since some hammers, when they get frightened, disappear completely, and once their re-spectability is gone, there won't be any banging, and that means less time in the shopping mall, where the mix of warm and cool is always just right, so that even when I enter menopause I won't have to carry around a handbag stuffed with spare blouses.

The fan at the entrance, between the doors that automatically slide open to welcome me in, messes up my hairdo, so it looks like, instead of walking, I took the train, leaning out the window the whole way. Lucky some drunk didn't throw a bottle and hit her in the head, the saleslady must be thinking, because if I had been hit by a bottle, instead of signing this credit card receipt for 4,560 crowns right now, I would be waiting in the emergency room for the nurses to finish eating their rolls and sew up my face.

Looking like that would be terrible. Everywhere I went I would have to explain how it happened, and men would pay

for my coffee and pastry without my even asking, but their hammers wouldn't hop up in their pants. I would feel sorry for them, too. Only hands free, with no blood pumped into them. Maybe the men would even lay a hand on my shoulder, where you touch people who are ugly and old, since there's no revulsion to overcome, even if they're sweaty or have eczema or no teeth, but to whisper in somebody's ear is less appealing, especially mine, on the side where a bottle went flying by and took a piece of my earlobe with it. In a few days, the birds on the railway embankment would be pecking away at it, and I would have gotten used to it being missing, but life is better having a nice face like this, and besides, I don't like getting used to anything new.

That's why, even though I don't like it one bit, I don't change anything in my room. Getting used to a room being nice, when that's how it actually ought to be, is more complicated than saying it's nice when it actually isn't. When on top of that, all the remodeling is done, there's nothing else you can think of, and the flat of your dreams is occupied by a series of unengaging visitors, who comment on every little thing and take down the dimensions of your new living room set on a piece of paper with a pencil stub casually pulled from their pocket as you read to them from the booklet that came attached to it. You don't have a measuring tape at home, so it becomes clear that you don't assemble your furniture yourself, unlike some of your less affluent friends, but that you have a man for that, at which point a conversation ensues. One of them

remarks that they would like to see that man, which doesn't mean that he would like to be introduced, but that you ought to find yourself someone, because you're thirty years old, and apart from pity or envy, a single woman of thirty isn't likely to encounter any other human emotions. This is the way people try to scare you to death as they jot down the dimensions of your incredibly comfortable furniture while they marvel, either quietly or out loud, at where you got the money for it.

That's why I don't intend to change a thing in the molded plastic room with the little yellow bird.

I call it that because there are three rooms in my flat, and if I said just "the molded plastic room," it wouldn't be clear which I meant.

Cuckoo

A lot of men who come to see me think that it's poetic. That I came up with the name "plastic three-room suite" just for our one special evening together, and now that little yellow bird of theirs is bobbing up and down impatiently in their pants, ready and waiting, like a whistle for me to slip in my mouth, and it knows it and is looking forward, trilling away at the thought, or like a mallet beating a drum and we'll spin and twirl to the rhythm, or just like a regular cuckoo, waiting inside the clock, and it won't strike until the timepiece in the little gamekeeper's lodge says so, and that's good also, it might even be the best.

Especially if it's a downy chick that grows really quickly. A clumsy big baby cuckoo that hatches in a nest full of little yellow birds and grows and grows and it's even surprised at itself, since nothing out of the ordinary is even happening yet, I haven't even laid a hand on him, and we'll spend a little while longer having a totally normal chat about his job in telecommunications, and I'm actually really interested in that at the moment, since my internet keeps going out, they probably don't value my business very much, and I'm just about to give the man my number when I realize that he already has it and stop myself mid-sentence. The kingdom of well-considered silences: That could very well work as the name for my suite of molded plastic rooms that evening, with the two of us as teensy Ken and fragile Barbie in our little pink molded plastic home. Enjoy it even more by looking down on us from a bird's-eye view, and thanks to the size of our little love nest, which is no larger than a shoebox considered from that perspective, you can have it all at your fingertips, like a sightseeing tour of the city by helicopter, and that's also about how much it would cost you to spend the night with me. By now he's got a hard-on. His is one of those big cuckoos that are timid at first, since they haven't had that much life experience yet, apart from throwing a couple fledglings out of the nest, but that was in the office of the telecommunications firm, and that can't be compared at all with the operation I run.

I think about how I'll go to get my internet taken care of, which like everything else in life is best handled through people you know, so instead of doing it over the phone, I'll take my hat with the peacock feathers and ring the bell downstairs like any ordinary customer who needs a question answered or a deeper understanding of the technical details. When I get to the reception desk, I'll ask to speak to him personally, the big cuckoo with the cuckoo hammer, which at that point will be drooping with no energy whatsoever, since that's what hammers do in offices, is droop. They only come to life in those brief moments when the new girl bends over to add paper to the copy machine and the paper drawer just refuses to close and keeps popping back out like a jack-in-the-box. His new coworker is totally soaked in sweat and she isn't even in menopause. It could be said that the flirting has already begun as the baton passes to the cuckoo, who gladly offers to help out his frustrated coworker with the luscious breasts and the cute little jacket that keeps them tightly confined, so they only bounce around a little and rub against each other even more as the cuckoo and his coworker together give it the two-handed slide.

As the paper drawer snaps shut in the warm and cozy little room, the paper is safely tucked away inside the purring copier, and the cuckoo is tucked away too, even though he would rather be the one sliding in, but his coworker just gives him a fleeting smile, too fleeting even for a noncommittal cup of coffee.

There actually was a chance to talk some shop at the vending machine in the hallway, but by the time he thought of it, it was too late, and his hammer, silly little thing, thinking they might actually have a chance, was seized with sadness at how easily she got excited every time, even though it was a lost cause. The same thing happened every day, so why couldn't it learn its lesson once and for all, and just stay in sleep mode the whole time, in between trips to the toilet?

The cuckoo, left alone again now, with no one but the copy machine, grumbling away as if it were just grumbling for effect, wonders whether his new coworker drinks cappuccino like all the other new girls before her, the ones trying to act classy, who also like it with the little foam on the top. The hammer considers giving a little hop as the cuckoo imagines his new coworker licking the foam from the cappuccino, lips swollen with pleasure, and maybe this time it wouldn't be just cappuccino foam, but the hammer's outpouring of joy. Except at the last minute the hammer changes its mind about hopping, remembering how useless it was just a while ago, so the cuckoo doesn't let out even the quiet groan he feels coming on as he imagines his new coworker with her face splattered in cum, too much for her to be able to lick it all up herself. Instead she would just helplessly roll those big doey eyes of hers while she blinked her eyelashes in surprise, as if this were her first time, a little bit of her mascara smearing in the sperm.

If he had been twenty, it would have been enough for him to get off again, but at forty probably not.

So, in the end, it would be a quiet sigh instead of a sensual groan that escaped the cuckoo's lips just before I knocked on the door to his office, at the very end of the hallway. It would be the timid knock of a young woodpecker just getting its bearings and not quite sure if it was this tree that needed help or the next one over.

In fact, if we've never been there before, we can never be sure whether or not we're knocking on the right door. If there isn't a nameplate on it, or a number, and the only description of it that we have came from the sweet but bored-looking temp receptionist at the front desk, who doesn't care how many times you knock on the wrong door, since in the end you'll find the right one, then afterward walk back out past her in mock haste, as if the whole thing were actually your fault, not hers, the tigress, just polishing her nails all day, clueless to company protocol.

So I knocked uncertainly, but at the same time sort of purring, if you know what I mean. When you're expecting someone and you can tell it's his knockity-knock from a hundred miles off by the way your heart starts pounding. And he would be ready too. Primed by the thought of his new coworker and her luscious breasts, even if he was engrossed in paperwork again, the knockity-knock would give him a thrill, since he would think it was her coming back, and if she'd come to ask him about toner for the printer, so he could help her push it in there, and after that an invitation for cappuccino would go without saying, because after all those years the cuckoo was

an expert in company come-ons, and this knockity-knock, coming right after their two-handed pushing the jack back in the box, was straight out of the company come-on handbook, and you would think the new girl might have been able to think of something more subtle than to interrupt just as he had finally managed to immerse himself in last year's financial statements.

Now all that's left is to hope that he isn't disappointed when he opens the door and sees me standing there, instead of the hot babe from the next department over, whose face he has just finally managed to recall. At first he's bound to be a bit surprised, no way around it, but a hammer never hops to attention so quickly as when it hasn't been informed in advance and, as a result, is obligated to improvise, so to speak. Similarly, the desk covered with last year's statements wouldn't have the slightest idea what it was about to be used for, even though in any case I doubt it would object. The chair too would probably be pretty bored at this point, trapped under the cuckoo's rear end the whole time, never mind that this man, choking in his tie and suit, has a first-class derriere, the likes of which are rarely seen on men who spend their days sitting. Even the most expensive rolling office chairs, with adjustable settings and armrests, will crush a shapely rear end flat.

Once we get under way, he's going to need those armrests, but meanwhile I just hand him my hat and walk in uninvited. The cuckoo has never seen a hat with peacock feathers before, not even outside of working hours, and the fact that I

just strolled right in without an invitation only adds to his bewilderment, and that's not even to mention his hammer, there's nothing going on down there just yet, the little pump remains just as the cuckoo decided it should be, ideally, between visits to the toilet. However, then I introduce myself and remove my coat, and we start to get a little activity down there, like a paramecium culture left on the windowsill over the radiator. The organisms may be imperceptible to the naked eye, but a strong smell wafts from the jar, heralding the birth of new life. I wouldn't pull the condom from my purse until just beforehand, in a casual, offhand way. That goes without saying. I don't use protection as a comic device with men I haven't met before, since the whole thing is too fragile and I feel that way myself. Like a snow queen made of glittering snowflakes and spider webs. Also, the cuckoo might wonder if the whole thing isn't just a delusion, but the moment I pressed his hand between my palms into my crotch, he would utter a groan identical to the one intended for his new coworker a few minutes earlier, putting an end to such idle thoughts, and the whole thing would continue on from there as it should. Tightly gripping one of his fancy office chair's armrests in each hand as if he were just on the verge, with my head between his knees he would be ready to get off. But I wouldn't let him. Not right away. Just little by little. And if he were to open his eyes, with his hammer angry red, protruding from his crotch like a blood-soaked bludgeon, I would lie down on the desk with my knees splayed wide and smile like Mr. Sunshine in a

magazine for young readers, and I think the exact expression on my face at that moment wouldn't be as critical as the one at the beginning, though I wouldn't want to overrate myself. Though I wouldn't want to underrate myself either. Anyway, endings are always a little bit sad and more like each other than beginnings.

The next day, ideally, he wouldn't be entirely sure whether or not it had been a dream. He would dig through the balance sheets in his wastebasket in vain for the protective sac filled with his spunk, since I would have taken it with me. Maybe on the threshold, assuming it was inside the office, since otherwise one of the employees' kids might pick it up, I could leave behind, as if I had forgotten it, the smallest one of the peacock feathers from my hat, so the cuckoo could caress himself with it afterward, some other day, when he had a brief moment free on the job, but the thought that he might cum on it dissuaded me from the idea, since the whole point of the scene was to be tender and cuddly, like my snowflake outfit, and sperm and the way my sticker-inner smacks his lips when he likes the taste of a meal are both part of my reality several times a week in my molded plastic three-room suite with kitchen, and they're there right now, back in my flat with the cuckoo, the customer is king. He's just a tad confused that I stopped in midsentence like that.

You see, he doesn't suspect a thing about my plan with the phone or, as I realize at the last minute, that he has my number, and he doesn't have the slightest inkling what just happened

in his office, and if it did actually happen, the cleaning lady who comes to empty the trash at the end of the day would rush right over to open the window, because the air in there would smell like after a coed aerobics class. By the way, the cuckoo keeps dumbbells under the binders in his office, and I like a man who takes care of himself. I know, even though I've never been to his office and no one is going to get me in there either, I soon recognize the cuckoo's body, and his muscles will be bulging as the hammer and the sticker-inner scrape out their song of joy. A bit out of tune, perhaps, given that it's the first night and the cuckoo, as you might expect, isn't completely over his stage fright yet, and I myself am not always in top form either. Still, on the whole it goes off without a hitch and on top of that I get the information on the new rates, and the very next day I change my plan based on the cuckoo's advice. For a long time I wanted to cancel my service completely, since apart from everything else, the mobile phone in my purse keeps buzzing, and sometimes at home, when I have a buzzer duet going on and don't know which way to turn first, I say to myself, This is one of those dilemmas I could certainly do without.

Having so many devices around that always ask to be treated kindly is the best way to end up annoyed. When a man calls, for instance, and it's a client, but all I see on screen is a number, no hammer or caller ID, and my negative attitude backfires on me. But anyway, thanks to the cuckoo's discounted rate, I ended up not cancelling any of my phones.

The really naughty hammers can sometimes get off from nothing but a phone call, even the initial contact conversation, which in theory should be no different from, say, calling information for the weather or an overseas number. Services like that also have part of their announcement recorded on tape, or, these days, probably more likely, a glossy-sleek e-disc, have you noticed? The lady they have in there is so sweet, with a voice that could definitely go places doing radio plays, or dubbing foreign commercials, which is financially more lucrative, but she just loves her work and wouldn't dream of giving it up for a well-paid position that didn't involve speaking with people but only to machines, and besides, it wouldn't help anyone as much as the weather hotline, which daily saves dozens, possibly hundreds, of young ladies from getting soaked in the rain and coming down with a chill, which might prevent them from going on a date the next day or, if the damp socks froze their feet, take away their appetite for bouncy-bounce with their boyfriend, and that would have dampened her spirits too.

These telephone women are the ones who advise us to wear a raincoat, or to pack sunscreen if you have skin type one, one plus, or two minus. In fact, it's best to have sunscreen on hand at all times. No one yet has died of excessive lotioning, and if I'm the first, I can add a Guinness world record to my list of achievements. Still, I would ask a few more years though. Thirty is just the gateway to adulthood, not a spout draining into a life you live to be rewarded. Though there are some nice

gentlemen who claim otherwise. All those cardinals and holy trinities, I can't keep the names straight. But if they've got part of their message recorded on tape too, I would tell this world it's one big scam, right to its face. Let the world work it out on its own, let it call a crisis intervention line for a change, instead of always just us, with our constant capriciousness and unpredictable moods.

The lady on the hotline got off to such a pleasant start, I had the feeling that she was genuinely interested in me, that maybe word of my renown had somehow reached them there at the central switchboard and she would want to know what it was really like when a woman is satisfied and isn't just faking it, but after getting off to such a pleasant start, I suddenly heard a click, like when you unbutton a snap on your coat.

For that matter, ladies can undress on the phone without fear, since most people don't have videophones, and even if some shameless lech were to call the information hotline on a videophone and that lady got him, a little light would start blinking warning her that something was wrong, and she would have time to get dressed before she got on with the ill-mannered caller, since you almost always have to wait on hold with a song until it's your turn. You can be sure that's the system they have down at the central exchange, they put it in place a long time ago, and my guess is they aren't likely to change it anytime soon.

The little red light that blinks when it doesn't like the looks of something recognizes not only calls from videophones, but

any number stored in its memory whose owner hasn't paid the bill in some time, and phones in abandoned houses or flats where there is a reasonable suspicion of criminal activity but the men from the police haven't yet had a chance to pay a visit in person, since they have plenty of other things to do too, though I'm forbidden from discussing them in any further detail, so in that way the switchboards also serve the men from the police as an auxiliary service.

Any phone call from a suspect number is automatically filmed and recorded in high definition, so that even in the case of alterations caused by chronic cold or momentary sleepiness, the suspect's voice sounds as clear as if he were whispering directly into the detective's ear. This ingenious interface between police forces and information services benefits all of us who would otherwise be left exposed to their ravages unprotected, so that sometimes they can also be of use to us.

Briefly put and to the point, after a pleasant conversation with the lady, I had a special little offer to propose for the two of us together right on the tippity-tip of my tongue, when I heard that click of the jacket snap and some freaking machine came on and started reciting the number I needed into the receiver, like the ones that announce the trains at the big railway stations, which in recent years have also become inhuman and e-, though traditionally they've served as humanity's greatest refuge. It used to be the level of discharge and secretions there was higher than the volume of oil that

a sturdy locomotive churns out over its wheels in the course of a shift, and instead of that now they've got these e-ladies and -gentlemen installed everywhere, dreadful, I tell you, sometimes it's enough to make even an optimistic person such as myself get depressed when the intonation at the station or over the phone doesn't drop in between the numbers or the names of the towns. Afterward it leaves me feeling like a German shepherd in obedience school, the ones they just bark commands at, and unless you happen to have a pencil handy you're out of luck, since they won't repeat the number back to you more than twice.

All this up to now is just an introduction, to make it clear what people are paying for when they come to me, and that it isn't actually an exorbitant sum at all, but on the contrary quite reasonable and, to overstate somewhat, ridiculously inexpensive when you consider the fact that it also includes my intonation, which some say is cuddly, even on the first visit, provided that I'm in the mood, although I always emphasize that whatever the men desire, they can do it again, and I can do the same again for them as well.

Naturally, some of the older men are a bit slower on the uptake or, so what, maybe they just don't hear that well anymore, and since I stand behind what I say on the phone, I'll say it a second time without a hint of impatient annoyance, which you can sense even on lines that aren't e- yet, but nobody at the central exchange gives a hoot about you anyway.

So even during those first few contact calls, which in terms of vocal range and mutual consideration should really be no different from the regular ones when men call with a similar urge to relieve themselves of something, except that during it their hammers just hang there quietly, without a peep, assuming, that is, that the man acts like a gentleman in everyday life, and not like a dick butting his nose in all over the place, ready to get off at the drop of a hat without permission, not only from the woman, but sometimes even from his owner himself. Those are more the medical cases, though, and while I do meet with them too, I don't especially seek them out, and I'm always glad when a case like that, instead of hiring my services, requests special assistance from the appropriate agencies, since that takes courage and, I'm sure, overcoming shame as well.

On the other hand, it means that I too have to deny myself something, namely some attractive item from the shopping mall, which is to say that I too practice self-abnegation, so both of us deserve recognition for that, as well as the items awaiting me in the shopping mall. They will just have to wait a little longer, no matter how fed-up they may be already, since they certainly have less reason than I do to enjoy the air, which is overly dry as a result of the air conditioning, but at least I can buy things amid the arid atmosphere, whereas they have to wait, long-suffering, until the milk of several men is converted into financial flows and my credit card is once again sufficiently paid up.

In fact, finances are essential to discuss in my initial phone contact with any man, although they ought to have informed themselves about it in advance. Still, I always repeat the menu, in a casual, offhand way, so that everything is settled and there's no back-and-forth once he flips out his hammer, which is understandably eager to go, because it's been a while now since the appointment was made and she isn't in the mood for any tug-of-war between her owner and the proprietress of the sticker-inner, which at this point is all she has in her small but rapidly growing head. On top of which, assuming the time is firm and there are no reschedulings, which overworked men and fathers with demanding families have a habit of, then quite possibly the hammer's owner hasn't polished it in quite some time, either by hand or in his wife, so that when his evening with me finally rolls around, he'll be as full as the tub filling with hot water while you take care of business, in my case a call with a client who'll come by later full to bursting. If you ask me, he might as well stuff it into the fat fiftysomething in accounting, the one who's been making googly eyes at him, since by that point the hammer would be happy with anything, and he wouldn't have to throw away his money on me, since I'm sure his children need new school supplies, a bike, and all those e-things they have nowadays, which are more expensive than anything else.

I can't tell the men that, though. They aren't paying me for advice, and I bet they wouldn't even say thank you, let alone

be grateful to me for trying to help them save money. It isn't anything other than pure altruism on my part, especially given that the sticker-inner prefers to spend most of his time relaxing, and when a hammer gives him a quick bang-bang, it's much more restful than those marathons with the ones who beat off just before they come over, or even right there on the spot, in my plastic three-room suite.

Sometimes they want me to watch while they do it, or moan along with them, which is no problem, but the second they ask for the slightest touch, I bill it as a separate pre-trick item, in which case they make two payments in the course of the evening, but I think, in view of the length and arduousness of the marathon of chafing my sticker-inner has to undergo with the hammer before she rises a second time, so that finally it can blow her horn, which coming so quickly after the first is rarely more than a little toot, for that kind of heroic work, I think I deserve double compensation.

Any man who refuses to fork over the cash he owes and then calls me a fucking bitch, even though it was a fair contract and he agreed to the terms and was informed of them in advance, had better take a look at his own flushed face and ask his hammer if it's worth it to her, and I think you can guess what her answer would be.

But it's her owner who's paying, and once he pays, the hammer just hangs there quietly again, like a sloth's tail, without a peep. The truth is, that sidekick of hers, whose sweaty crotch she's attached to at the root, is closer to her than I am,

or general justice, never mind that I'll soon satisfy her and that it's only thanks to me that she'll soon be drifting off so happily into la-la land. Despite all this, and despite that in her honest little head, hammers for the most part being far more upright than their owners, she may suspect an injustice is being committed against me, still, blood is thicker than water and so the hammer plays possum. She plays possum even when her owner punches me in the face, though she does do a little skip, give a cheer and poke her head out, curious about the ruckus, because hammers tend to be curious and some of them really like violence, and even the jaded old frankfurters, whom I would least expect it from, snap right back after that.

When it comes to the contact call, it goes without saying the violent ones are just as pleasant or unpleasant as any of the rest, in fact I would even say they tend to be somewhat more pleasant in terms of their voice, at least judging by the fact that the ones who are vulgar at first are often the sweetest little ladybugs once they undress, and want to turn off my big overhead sixty-watt bulb and stretch out beside me like we were in a meadow, or lying on the rug in his parents' living room getting ready to listen to records, instead of here in my molded plastic fuckshop, where there's no need to waste time with any of that.

The attentive ones might spend the first few minutes, say, caressing my silhouette with the palm of their hand, ever so lightly fluffing my tits, biding their time before taking another

tiny step, moving closer to me and into me, even though their hammer has been standing at attention for a good long while now and nothing has prevented her from disappearing into that greased oven, where she wants to be more than anywhere else, much sooner. For some reason, however, her owner is stalling, and the reasons are various.

But the number of true shrinking violets who come to me is low. The ones whose ears blush when a woman's shoulder strap slips off, or who can't imagine it without foreplay, or can imagine it but that's all, since no woman has ever spoken to them about the other options, and due to their shrinking nature they themselves would never start anything, so they may not even realize that, right in their very own building, just one floor down, beneath their bedroom, they have a fuckshop with a flexible sticker-inner. Not that he's missing out on anything all that great. As a matter of fact, the men who choose to do without it, being above it all, and even if sheerly out of genuine embarrassment, have nothing but my respect, but they aren't my customers and no financial benefits flow from their milk to my card. The type with whom my only experiences are purely private, and, in comparison with my professional ones, those are negligibly few.

The few true shrinking violets who have come to see me have usually received it as a gift for their birthday or somesuch, assuming something as stupid as an experience you don't care for can be called a gift, since even though a lot of men dream of going to a prostitute, there are men who don't care for it,

and with them it's better to agree the terms in advance, since it's a sure thing the idiot who bought it for the poor guy will call me up the next day to see how it went, and his hammer will be trickling the whole time we're having our conversation, till he's done talking to me and runs off to the bathroom for a sec to blow himself.

An investment like that in your coworker, where, standing in my doorway, he and I agree on whatever I roped the idiot into when he called, makes even less sense than coming the moment the tip of your hammer touches my sticker-inner, when that fat fiftysomething from accounting could just as well replace me. That way, my sticker-inner would be spared the scraping, the woman would probably come for joy at screwing a sharp-looking guy my age, and he would save himself the payment, which, for that matter, like almost nothing else in my private life, I would keep all to myself.

So if you're looking mainly for information of that nature, because your hammer would enjoy a hop in the sack with a whore, but you aren't sure whether you have the savings for it, instead of giving your hammerdehoy a bit of an airing out while you have a little chat with me, I suggest you pick up some porno mags on the way home from the office, the back page is all you need, you don't even have to buy it, or at night, after the wife and kids have gone to sleep, just click around the web.

Sadly enough, the ones who never make it to my molded plastic fuckshop tend to be the very homebody type I'm

describing here, whose only regret is any expenditure of effort or money. I wouldn't be saying this if they sank the money from their tedious office job into their child's school supplies, even if their lousy fifty crowns might end up in a Coke machine or a video game, since, after all, even adolescents have the right to a good time. Especially since their little hammers and sticker-inners aren't fully developed yet, so they probably shouldn't be using them. They should wait a little longer, till things get stronger and fill in with hair and rise like bread, although the young ones all too often lack patience for that, which then leads to premature tearing and ejaculation, although thank God not new and even more-miniature children.

Company Lunch

Lastly, and we ought not to forget them, we have the wives. I'm surprised they didn't start pushing for their rights sooner, seeing as they're so emancipated that they want to wash dishes only on Mondays, Wednesdays, and Fridays, even when the whole thing boils down to nothing but switching on the control panel of one of those great big dishwashing units. For too long now, their screaming voices have been noticeably missing here. The legitimate aggrievedness of those who nearly singlehandedly wrestle the whole household machinery up the punishingly long hill of family life, an uphill climb that may last far longer than the women ever dreamed of, even back in their teenage

nightmares, when the very idea of family was a horror of horrors, and suddenly it was their one happiness, even if at times it was also a real pain in the neck. But often it's all that women have got. When they do a reorganization at work, you're out the door before you can blink, there's not even time to pack your bag of decaf from the kitchen nook, where you and your coworkers had such a nice time gossiping in the mornings, even if it didn't boost your performance in any way. Doing without a woman's care around the family hearth is far more difficult than it is in manufacturing work, so the boss at home has to think twice about casting a woman out of the nest, especially when it's supplementally insured by contracts and lovelaced promises.

But it doesn't always work out even here, and at least part of the time, it absolutely definitely isn't the woman's fault at all.

Whoever wants, can now throw their hands up in horror or start crying over the milk, in case it happens to be about to spill at your house, although nowadays it comes across as a bit outdated, and the old-world ai yi yi's aren't suited at all to the modern woman.

Suited or not, our figures slacken with age, even in our sleep, and even I know, when mornings I go for a run along the riverbank to combat my advancing wrinkles, which are still pretty cute for now, that eventually time will catch up with me, and besides there isn't a way to run in your sleep, you just keep right on aging, no matter how sweet your dreams are. And that's not to mention those of us who, between raising children and wiping dust, don't have time to run. Especially if no nice

lady comes to their home to help out, like the service I pay for, now there's an ai yi yi for you. So instead of a package of markers that erase at one end and leak on the other, daddykins could buy something to lift the spirits of that special someone with whom he pledged to spend the rest of his life, even if maybe when they stood there signing the piece of paper he didn't totally mean it. Run right through with Cupid's arrow, it was just about all he could do not to bungle the flowers, or maybe he had to get married, so he was better off not giving it too much thought, it was bad enough that they were going to live with his mother-in-law and his friends gave him a bit of a razzing about it, too. Still, the banknotes he would rather be stuffing into my panties often end up going to his wife anyway. Either in the form of some slyly planned vacation with a demi-pension, or at the very least an anniversary bouquet, with some dopey inscription saying how many years they'd stuck it out together, so she would know he remembered. Women, I'm sorry to say, are partial to that kind of thing, since it makes them feel that they're being taken care of and that their welfare is better provided for if their husbands remember not only the bills and new shoes for the children, but also a regular reckoning of their years together in matrimony. As if relationships ripened like wine.

Meanwhile the truth is they're more like distilled water, which you can use just as easily to make saltwater gargle as strawberry juice, though I can't imagine who would want to spit out their own marriage.

But at least just as often the daddykins go and squander their finances on things that a public broader than an audience of one will appreciate, for example, auto accessories. And not only those that contribute to safety, such as snow tires and new brake pads, which I understand as much as I do the money children fritter away on entertainment instead of a pair of those ugly orthopedic sandals, but also on useless e-objects, which I don't understand and which in my view are of no use to a family. And if this daddykins is thinking of me as he sticks it into his wife's barely wet sticker-inner, or of some other as yet still classified pussy that he could be sticking it in without any big getting to know each other and buying trifles, the way that you have to when something happens with a coworker on a business trip, then he isn't a man of principle, but a lazy little shit, which most of my timidistas are. The kind who, when he comes to me, it's his first time paying money for it, even though he's going on forty. Who up until then had been hoping that a mail order service might deliver a new pussy straight to his desk and at most he would have to go pick it up at the post office. Or maybe they could bring him one at that cheap restaurant where he paid for his lunch every day using MoneySaver meal vouchers with a feeling of terrific savings, served up on a plate instead of his usual pork and dumplings, and the fresh cunt would peel itself open for him right there on the spot, presenting itself for inspection like it was posing on a stepladder in a porno photo shoot, then jam itself down onto his tool, throbbing red and dribbled with soup, all the

way to the hilt. He would come almost immediately, given that surprise invariably causes a rapid increase in blood flow, belch a little onion soup into my hair, and the matter would be strictly settled. Of course the waiter would have hung a little sign outside in advance to say the place had been booked for a private function, and in the event that it was prolonged to include, say, intercourse with some of his coworkers seated at the table with him, who would be duly pre-informed of our performance, with one of the younger ones fleeing to the men's room even before I was through with the first, or at least to the coatrack, to find some peace and quiet, the whole thing could be camouflaged from management as an abruptly scheduled lunch with a client of the firm, and it wouldn't be totally lying either, since even if they're the clients according to my rules, on the other hand I'm the client of their wallets.

It would be a bit disappointing if all they had in their bill-folds were MoneySaver vouchers and some photos of their children. It's only the lack of finances that would upset me, needless to say. They can carry around fistfuls of pictures for all I care, kids, landscapes, whatever they want, as long as it doesn't get in the way of their paying. But with this squad it probably would, I doubt they could throw together enough to afford me on their lunch break just off the cuff like that.

The main hitch as I see it, though, is all the other people who would be in there having lunch when they brought me out on the plate. I realize it can be a lot more laughs banging a pussy for hire with a gang of buddies than all by yourself in

some rancid cubicle with a little red lantern, the way people imagine a love nest to look when they haven't seen my molded plastic three-room suite, still nobody likes having total strangers, some bums they wouldn't even share a table with for lunch and would wait instead for a seat to open up somewhere else, staring at their prong the whole time they're having sex. No one except those special few, who I'm glad when they take their unimpressive childhood issues directly to a doctor instead of trying to work it out by way of my sticker-inner.

Also, having so many gawkers present from outside the department, where the awareness of complicity would bind all parties to secrecy, lest word get back to the wives, would mean a risk of a leak of information that ideally would remain the object of suggestive references exclusive to members of the gentleman's club. Said club, of course, having been informally established that same afternoon by way of this unforgettable experience, and I would bet my neck the men will spontaneously celebrate the anniversary every year, and even if some forget, surely there will be one to commemorate the occasion by sending a funny text to everyone in the old gang who hasn't changed their number, and maybe attach a racy image, which he could easily find on the web with a little due diligence.

I think you will acknowledge that comparing this to dashing out to the florist before they close to pick up a bouquet for a wedding anniversary is like comparing apples and grapefruit, and even if I don't know what goes with what, by virtue of my sizable tits, I confidently declare myself to be grapefruit.

This doesn't solve the question of how to send those annoying gawkers packing, but that's what waitstaff are for, and once they had successfully carried out their assignment, they would be more than welcome to take a turn as well. Surely they would have more in the till than that squad of nonentities from the company had in their wallets, and cheap restaurants with high turnover in personnel are used to shortfalls in cash.

TV Episode Two:
The Fatness of Old Ladies

The moment a client is out the door, it's over. He takes the tram in time to catch the midnight telenovela and get a few quick z's in before the alarm goes off, and I'm free. I don't share my plastic three-room suite with any man in between. Nor would I be able to keep something so important as a man at home all my very own a secret for long, and I was about to say "not to brag," but there's no way I could know if he would be something to brag about. Though assuming I chose him, then obviously yes, since no bump on a log would get so much as his thumb across my threshold outside of working hours, and besides, just snaring a solid unspoken-for man at thirty is

something to brag about. At least according to the traditional-minded ladies you see cluster together in every building, and in mine they've gotten into the habit of turning to look at me, the whole bunch of them at once, whenever I walk past.

People with a surplus of free time learn all sorts of things, including how to turn in unison in a circle of friends, although it's possible these ladies had picked it up back in the days of the Spartakiades. They certainly looked Communist enough, and they didn't take synchronized swimming class. I've never seen any of them with wet heads, so they didn't learn their teamwork there.

I suspect they've got an inkling that there's more to my plastic three-room suite than is written in the housing association records. There are so many boxes on those forms that a little word like fuckshop could easily be hidden in there amid the forest of squiggles. Which is to say, it could be there without anyone discovering it and I would have a clear conscience, but also someone might discover it and then I'd be in all sorts of pickles and jams, as I'm sure they refer to problems when they huddle in their cluster, using the term from back in the days of the Communist sons of bitches, when you got into jams whatever you did, and with all their plotting and scheming, the women were like the big bad wolf threatening to lead us back into the deep, dark past.

I know it would help if I got to know them better, since deep down inside their kitchen coats, which are probably raincoats, since they're artificial fabric, so they offer good

protection against not only rain but grease, deep down inside, at their core, the women are softhearted, but to get through all those tons of bacon to their inner core would be one heck of a slog, I don't even know if you could pound your way in with a hammer, but I'm not about to tell them to try it out at my place, even at a discount I couldn't get a client for one of those beefy retirees, in fact I'd be lucky to walk away with anything more than a slug in the face. A bruise is like an infectious disease, like a crow, when one sits down there's always another one coming, and number three is waiting right around the corner. I guess a blue face gives men the courage to make it even bluer, and afterwards I have to rinse the bad taste out of my mouth with a truly enormous purchase using the money they paid to spray their loads. So big I have to make two trips home from the shopping mall or go by car, but usually I make two trips, since I don't realize ahead of time that my purchases will add up to such a gigantic pile.

It's like the little gifts I give myself have tiny little hands that caress my battered cheeks, and the face that recuperates with love is the one that recuperates fastest, and lickety-split, in just a few days, my shop window is good as new, which it has to be, if I don't want to lose my clientele.

The cluster of retirees might be relieved not to have so many men wandering the hallways with their shirttails untucked, but they aren't about to slip an envelope with a thousand crowns under my door, since they're other people's grandmothers, not mine, which is why they don't feel bad for their harsh

opinions of me and stick them into the less-used drawers at the back of their heads the way they do for their strung-out darling little granddaughters, for whom I'm sure they can always find a thousand crowns, even if then old granny has to spend the rest of the week boiling a chicken head. How to get fat on so little money, that's their most closely guarded secret and also mystery number two on my TV series. May I remind you, our first episode revolves around the question of whether anyone cares that menopausing women, by carrying heavy handbags filled with blouses so they can reclothe their sweaty bodies over the course of a day, firm up their bodies as a result of the effort they expend. Our TV crew is curious whether anyone will truly genuinely care or if nobody will give a fig, since firm or unfirm, old is old and worn-out no matter how you slice it. That's what I say, anyway, that those old ladies are just jealous of me when I cast the evil eye back at them, they were the ones who started it, not me, so I hope my evil thoughts, which after all sprouted from their evil seed, will get a pass in the great reckoning of Jesus Christ and the Holy Trinity.

Those gravy-stained lardasses would actually be amazed at how conservative and traditional I am when I feel like it. And I feel like it every day. Practicing a profession undoubtedly more traditional than anything their counter windows and offices, except the cuckoo's, have ever seen, because the mall I feed my money into is as greedy as a love-stricken sticker-inner, so I have to stay busy.

I would be hard pressed to find time for a man all my very own. No such man lives here, so no mutual soaping of bellies takes place in my bathroom, which serves exclusively as a latrine for clients. Whenever their bladders need vacating, I go in and clean up after them the moment they're gone. Once their juices spill over into my credit card, I see no reason to preserve their smelly toilet stains, although I make a point of telling them they're welcome to avail themselves of my commode before they leave, and after they arrive as well, to help them feel at home. Though if any of them actually were to start to feel that way, I would chase him out with a broom like the caretaker woman who huddles with all the rest of the bunch in my building, and I'm willing to bet that if any one man were to hang around my place on a regular basis and were to be frequently seen visibly walking the hallway, and how else would he do it, since he wouldn't be some carnival magician who walks through walls, anyway if he were seen around a lot, I bet then my three-room suite wouldn't stick in those women's craw anymore. And there could easily be things going on in there that would set even my most hardened clients' hair on end. Say, an after-school dance group for all their offspring, which the randy daddycats can use as an alibi to claim that they were over at their kid's little buddy's, on the off chance the little rascal at home should happen to ask where they were out so late. The scenes of all the daddykins gathering the kids together in a circle as one by one they rang my buzzer using the client's special ring while the kids' fun and

games continued in full swing, followed by the lovely family reunions, wouldn't offer anything mysterious for me to use in my TV series, but still, I could shoot it as a home video and sell it to the wives for a fortune. And if I had a love man all my very own here with me in my bath, who was sympathetic and understood this whole thing as the epilogue to the past life of his bride to be, with a punchline for the kids and a moral for the dads who think that little pitchers have little ears, so out of sight, out of mind, that love man of mine would jump right in the middle of the ring-around-the-rosy of gregarious kids and their daddykins, and they would be virtually connected to all the lonely mummies at home, and it would be just like a videoconference, only someone would have to visit all the moms ahead of time to make sure they knew to log on.

Still, it seems like a dirty trick, the whole thing stinks of crookedness, though I'm not quite sure yet which positions to put them in, maybe the daddykins clients bending the rosy over the window ledge, so the mummies bursting into the flat wouldn't catch them in flagranti. My sticker-inner would be properly cleaned, of course, as would the entire flat, for the sake of the children's hygiene and the safety of pedestrians, since little kids love to fill condoms with water and throw them off the balcony.

A hammer that can pound my sticker-inner flat as a cutlet isn't just something I lack at home in the form of a man all my very own, who would sit on the edge of my tub in the steam from

the hot water, since it isn't just peeping toms who like to ogle well-proportioned women in the shower through the suspiciously transparent glass of skylights, or paying clients, but also loving men. Of course a hammer can also be unattached at the loins, and in that case have nothing in common not only with a loving man but men in general, and a penile tool like that is what we call a toy. That's probably too long-winded an explanation, in light of what I wanted to say, which is simply that my three-room suite is also absent one of those. I don't have one. No dildo, no vibrator. No self-erecting quiverstick, manless wang, pond paddle, sleepytime tingletron, ticklepink for beddy-bye. I don't know why, but the more I think about it, the more dildos strike me as tender, almost girlish, even though I know little girls are predestined for more than just rubbing their pussies alone in their beds, or using a cute little teddy bear paw, which might lose one of its furry hairs in her undeveloped sticker-inner and give her an itch.

And yet, even despite dildos' girlishness, which personally I find appealing, I don't have a single one in the fuckshop, not even a whit of a one. If not me, you might ask, who else would keep a self-combobulating ding-dong underneath her pillow or stuck in an unfinished book on the nightstand to mark her place, am I right?

I can feel the electric charge in the air, and I know that it isn't a storm blowing ozone my way, but your lost voices answering back, which may be your way of indicating that something is highly unlikely, in this case a pussy without a

dildo. Just try to tell someone that they look about as credible as a pussy without a dildo and they'll get it right away. Well, that someone is me, and for the first time now I kind of feel like crying, because I might be losing your trust here.

So let's be clear. Every one of these relationships that I build depends on trust the way a baby kangaroo depends on its mama's teat, that's how strong the attachment is, and if you want to call my fuckshop a sac, like the one that embryos grow in, then you can go right ahead, since they both have all kinds of room for all kinds of things, but either way the baby kangaroos who ring my buzzer using the client's special ring so they can come and spray their jizz in or around my sticker-inner are the foundation, and the firm udder of my pussy, which they can grab and hang onto, is the cornerstone, without which no fuckshop, no matter how many rooms it has, will ever get off the ground.

I probably should have been a schoolteacher, but that's just an aside to the fact that I'm the one who holds the reins and the baby kangaroos jump to my tune, at least until some of them turn violent when they suddenly see through it all. The fact that the trust that forms the basis of our relationship is just an act, which they would have seen right away if their vision hadn't been clouded by the nebula of their cum like the glass people refer to using the slightly naughty term frosted, when it's really just plain cum-spattered. It's usually no big deal, as long as they don't become indisposed, which tends to happen to bullies, who don't swear up and down because

their dick is so big and wants it so bad, but because by nature it's actually an easygoing toothpick that takes almost as long to get up as a cripple knocked from his wheelchair. And not even using two legs or all fours, but from one single root that has to hoist the whole thing up by itself, since that's all it's got. No transmission, no wheel turned by a pair of devoted oxen like a mill for grinding grain. So when these types get indisposed, my confidence in the ultimate success of their as yet ungrowing but surely soon-to-ascend voluminousness comes in tremendously handy. In fact in these cases it's an absolute necessity, in order to ensure that anything happens at all and that the party favor even gets unwrapped in the first place. Like a rapier, like a pistol pow-pow, like a peace pipe handed across the circle of the fraternity of men who sow their seed far and wide, like a war pipe, provided we want a little drama, which on the one hand every little stinger poking out possesses inherently, and on the other, it needs in order to poke out sufficiently. This is why, in bed with the wife, the average hammer would rather just bundle up and snuggle close to the thighs of her owner, because those kinds of nice little cozy domestic tea parties lack even the slightest tinge of drama, so they quite often end in a state of inglorious mush, and as a result those men end up with me, because they want to attain glory and I'll help them as best I can.

It's a difficult situation when the drama just isn't there, and even after I bring to bear the full range of my skills and, playing the geisha, fan the drama with my fan like the hot breath of a

steamy mare, still nothing happens. I may even go so far as to put my hands on my hips and say, Sorry, but I'm no therapist, though it's better without the hands on the hips, since, unless the client's express wish is otherwise, I prefer to exercise my authority via covert means, and faced with a man in a state of nervous disarray, the hands on the hips can either frighten him out of the stable instability of his appendage, or, on the contrary, provoke aggression, which means bruises, and I don't want those, and I'm also no farmer's wife.

Under no circumstances do I want to give the impression that I enjoy it, because as soon as I say that my clients give me a slap in the face every now and then, I can already see those meat-beating hands wrap around their hammer, and not only do they get stiff when they imagine violence, but even more blood rushes to them if they imagine my pussy enjoys it too.

There are moments when I'm scared out of my wits, you bet your life I am. When I deserve a medal for bravery, though I don't know if I could use that to pick myself something up at the mall, they probably wouldn't take bravery per se, but whether it could be converted to money as easily as cum-shots are, I'm not sure about that either. In case anyone was wondering whether the money's the most important part, then yes, it is.

Anything else? No, nothing. But that nothing extends like a snake, like a sea of sand soaked with water, and that makes me think of my sticker-inner again, since when a songfest is a

success it ends up with a ton of water in there, and the cycle just keeps repeating like that, going round and round. This one gets turned on by money, that one by a smack in the face, and another one by a slab of beef as red as a cock all jacked up and ready to blow with its tip polished to the brilliant shine of a patent leather shoe. Pity they don't have red at the shopping mall, though they've got whole orchards of black models to choose from.

The polished shine on the stud who gets his rocks off in a minute reminds me of an angry turkey, except for that little teeny crystal droplet on the tip, which no fowl would ever wear. And one more thing. In case you haven't noticed, once that tool climbs on board, there's no riling him. He'll do whatever you want at that point, just as long as you let him in, that's all he cares about. In there where there's no talk and the two of them can finally can get down to work, which is also the reason why people join up in pairs, and even in multiples.

Do I ever invite in a partner as a bonus for good boys? You want to grab your tool and wag his head back and forth till he slobbers all over himself and make him talk like a puppet? Shame on you. And you like being a little boy? A naughty boy who needs to be punished? I just babble on like the radio, whatever it takes to stir the imagination of the men who have never fucked a stranger's pussy for money before, and I know there's plenty of you out there and you're normally an entertaining companion, but right now, all of a sudden, you're at a bit of a loss. In particular you aren't sure if you're

a wallflower decent man with values, or a wallflower wuss, who hopes they can bring me in on a plate like they did for the squad at the company lunch the other day. I'm not being flippant, and none of you were supposed to actually answer that question above, about the little boy being punished, not even in your mind.

Mea culpas on me, that was just a little teaser scene. A sneak preview before we begin, to help me gauge the mood. After that, I can reach into my bag of tricks, depending on which category the man falls into, all the general guidelines tell us is which chamber the two of us are going to peek inside. The one he likes the best, or the one he's never been in.

Whether a man is the exploring type, or just wants to reheat the conjugal bed with a new pussy, that's his business. I'm not here to retrain anyone, but to make do as best I can with as few words as possible, assuming talking isn't an agreed part of the routine. No matter how fat and covered in scabs he is, I wrap myself around him like velvet, that's my job. I get as close as I can to what they want, though generally they broadcast it before we even begin. Their bodies scream their desires. I'm telling you, the moment men set foot inside my molded plastic three-room fuckshop, they turn into a loudspeaker, because they can, just because. I don't know about the soul and all that hogwash, but it wouldn't do me any good if I knew anyway, I can tell you that. It's the same with the dildo, which I glossed over, but not intentionally, so any man who thinks he caught me in some double-dealing whore's little white lie that now

I'm trying to talk my way out of, can go belch about it down at the pub and come back once he's learned some manners.

Like I said, it runs on trust.

So are you sure you don't want to write down my phone number, not even on a teensy-weensy scrap of napkin with a teensier-weensier pencil? That way it would be almost like it didn't even exist, and by the time you pulled it out of your pocket after a few sweaty stops on public transit, all that would be left of it was a little ball of shreds, like when you run a hundred-crown note through the wash in the pocket of your jeans. You can't even get anything at the convenience store for that, never mind the mall. And even with a fresh new note, about all you can buy there for that's a hair band, which is why I've got to keep busting my butt.

On my own in my three-room flat, I simply make do with my fingers. My busybody little fingers, moving at high speed as if they were counting bills, only right in front of the entryway into my sticker-inner, the black hole with the cushions and the soft lacework around it.

The reason I mention bills isn't because I think about money while I'm doing it, honestly I don't, not even when I'm with a man in all my glory, but the motion is similar to counting bills, and any attempt to explain the self-gratifying ruffling of my wrinkly folds absolutely cries out for comparisons from daily life. Waxing poetic about the moon and aromas blossoming in the mist isn't part of my repertoire, even for an encore.

Your fingers ought to be clean, just as a side note for beginning girls, since actual bills would smudge them like a newspaper hot off the press. Nor do I advise the young masters to polish their little hammerlings with ink-stained fingers either, although reading the paper may produce the urge to do so, particularly if they page to a full-color photograph of an especially well-developed war correspondent and succumb to the yearning to rub one out for relief.

Then again, a hammer can withstand more dirt, since, unlike its counterpart, it isn't a window onto the boudoir of the body, but just the opposite, an escape hatch, its snake eye spitting on the ones it is most fond of, opening like a cuckoo clock operated by timer with a manual switch, set to go off when the testicles are full, like a clock when its big hand reaches the twelve, though of course a man can be induced to ejaculate even if he's less than full.

Whether or not I'm full depends on my mood, since I'm a woman and women are more psychological than physical, so they say. It's true I'm not nearly as strong as the average playboy and I melt the moment my lace is properly ruffled and wet as a wreath of fresh flowers, woven amid the morning dew, assuming we want to have a bit of fun with our girlishness, or wet as a dachshund that waddled under the rainspout, if we want to be firm and affirm that beads, ribbons and rings are ill-suited to the job description of fucking the living daylights out of a sticker-inner, and they aren't fit to stick in there either, since when you drop

something down that pitch-black pipe, it hurts and it can be hard to find.

Counting bills offers a woman more than enough self-gratification, and the agility comes with age, or sometimes right away, if there's a shortage of privacy, which of course, being all alone in my molded plastic three-room flat, is not an issue for me, but this description is meant to be a little for everyone, and it is.

In the Archive

To say that I'm traditional and old school makes it sound as though I walk around with my hair in a schoolmarm's bun, in a blouse of softened plastic and a skirt that blows against the wind instead of with it, being resistant not only to men, but also to the elements, which are also masculine in a way and inclined to disturb fragile things. To put it simply, some professions are no bed of roses. They don't add to your sex appeal, or so people say.

All those poor women librarians and archivists, always working on their card catalogs, rarely on themselves, and judging men by their glasses—if you have the same shape as

she does, it improves your chances, or so people say. It's not fair that these professions, unlike hospital nurses or temp secretaries or au pairs, almost never appear in porn magazines. Archivists can certainly be just as young as all the rest of them. What else would they do in the years between training and middle age except sit around in their offices looking young and fresh? No one else is going to do the work for them, and besides, there are plenty of hiding places in among the stacks, and what other job can you think of where it's so easy to pop out for a bit? That means instead of the man waiting awk-wardly at the door with a bouquet out in the rain, he could be right behind a bookshelf in the very same room, and could be watching the archivist enter data for a long time before anything happened, and the archivist could be writing one man's fantasies on scraps of paper by hand, poor overexerted thing, and another man's fantasies on a computer, she knows how she likes it best, but either way, a typewriter is the most delicate method.

A woman at a typewriter is gentle but with authority, part newly hired apprentice, part police detective, and in my mind this is the woman sitting there in the archive.

Not that I mean to force anything on you, but the reality is, I often know better than you what's best, and that isn't pride speaking, it's my profession. Now, managing a car wash efficiently, that's your department. Ditto stock prices, or even political news, that should also do the trick in case your mem-ber, after swelling at the thought of the archivist, might be

starting to deflate, because you don't work in either the stock exchange or the carwash business and you're concerned that as a result she may not think as highly of you, in which case our scene might be less than a tour de force, assuming of course an ever so slight to moderate degree of disdain doesn't appeal to you, since if you want me to kick you in the face with a tall studded black leather boot and call you a fucking sick piece of shit, then I'm sorry to say but you fall under specialty requests, or at any rate close enough to it that we would have to shake hands and part ways. Or I might stick it out with you to the end, although seeing you get it up would really get my goat, since it would take all kinds of kicks and insults, which is perverted. Maybe the only thing good about it is then my sticker-inner would get a little vacation, since it wouldn't be as plundered and pillaged after the session as it is after the clients who have a thing for marathons, as is often the case, and then in between working hours I have to devote extra special attention to it and cram it full of sticky treats.

Perhaps at this very moment our archivist is munching away on something sweet, to help make her work at least a bit enjoyable, it's the best way to safeguard against careless mistakes, but she's still a bit bored all the same, which ensures that even if you're not the studliest stud, you'll still be a pleasant break from routine. You've got a head, legs and arms, right? There wouldn't be room for a wheelchair in between the shelves, and that's where you'll have to go, even if you're a bit shy. In that case, however, you're just a sham shrinking

violet, since we've already had much harder stuff than this, prongs and dirty words, and you read this far, and now all of a sudden you don't want to knock on the door of a researcher in the Academy of Sciences' Institute of Oriental Languages? Meanwhile she's been expecting you all morning, looking up from her desk just in case you might walk in the door, and she's freshly washed, because even with such a demanding job she's one of those women who also takes care of themselves from the waist down, even though that part sits beneath the desk and nobody sees it, so she doesn't have to, but wet in clean panties is not at all the same thing as wet in dirty ones, and you might not find them so appealing either, since even luxury panties smell once they get old, and we have to get this foul mess out of the way so we can finally give the little hammer a tickle, since by now she might be starting to wonder what happened to that tasty delight she was promised and whether the whole thing isn't a con and a trap and she was driven into the stacks so someone could ambush them and chop her off, some embittered woman, say, who wanted nesting, not hammering, and instead the hammer banged her down to the bone, then drove off, attached to its owner, back to his wife, before sunup.

Blaming people for life's silly mishaps is one of those women's hobbies, like pulling the children's bedroom door all the way closed at night, or turning out the living room light even though the man will be coming home soon, so he has to grope along the walls until he finds the light switch while she

stands in a cloud of steam ironing his shirt again, so she can't be blamed. Nor can she be blamed for the foul mess with the soiled underwear, though she could have been more careful, long-term monogamous relationship or not, and she certainly can't be blamed for the embittered woman ready to pounce on your back with a knife from the shelf of eighteenth-century Japanese poetry, known for its brevity, since any true Japanese poet of that era visited a geisha at least three times a day, and concentrated work is impossible with the day chopped into pieces like that. For the time being, however, the woman saboteur perched on the shelf has forgotten her intention to deprive you of your member, her attention, like yours, suddenly drawn elsewhere.

Drawn to the archivist, who has suddenly ceased clacking away on the typewriter, popped the last treat from the dish into her mouth and, licking her lips, had an excellent idea. With her delicate little fingers, she has begun to unbutton her satin blouse, an article of clothing that, perhaps more than any other, stirs a desire to feel the heft of the breasts contained within it. Their full-bodiedness makes you long to see if they'll spill from your hands like little baskets filled to overflowing and to see if they both weigh exactly the same or one is a wee bit more developed than the other, although the little nipper needs caressing just as much as the fuller blossom, maybe even more, to appease him, so he won't feel sorry for himself and his nipple will harden just as quickly and compliantly. So now that your hammer has finally had

a good shaking-up, you step up from behind and, cupping her tits in your hands, give a squeeze and softly rub and she groans, but softly enough so the manager in the office next door doesn't hear, since he comes here to do this too, and he wouldn't be happy to meet you. For that matter the feeling is mutual, but don't worry. It isn't going to happen, don't even give it a second thought as you churn her breasts like a hot tub with a special whirlpool setting, which you'll be climbing into with another woman, but for now all the others to come are forgotten, as are all those from the past, who have suddenly faded from memory, banished by the archivist to the posteriormost lobe of the brain, where we store the junk we don't need to act out our fantasies, and lo and behold, this Wednesday the archivist has no underwear on, just a long, flowing Korean skirt, which is revealed when she stands, and now your cock is standing too, even more stiffly than her, and the only parts of her capable of that are her legs and breasts, now protruding so insistently that they practically seem to be begging, and a plea like that, to wedge yourself up and underneath a Korean silk skirt into the ass of a ready and waiting woman, could be rejected only by the shrinkingest of shrinking violets with the most unwavering principles, which he would have to repeat to himself, over and over, spinning the thought in his mind like the wheels on a stationary bike that it was healthy, although where health is concerned, there's nothing more beneficial than a thorough purge of bodily fluids, which you happen to be full of, and without delay, because,

given your state of readiness, any delay would result in your being cranky, if nothing were to happen, and it's happening right now. Relief, clenched between her cheeks, relief that the woman has been overpowered and nothing now can take her away, or take back what has happened, and given that she herself has begun to feel a bit embarrassed, without attempting to take a step back, since that would be the most awkward of all, and also you might get angry, and since she doesn't know you, she doesn't know what that would look like, she holds still like a little animal while you pump away, and every now and then you glance out the window to relieve the pressure in your hammer, since if you kept your eyes fixed on her glistening ass beneath the skirt you would come instantly, and now it's time and nobody's going to walk in, you think to yourself, since you don't know about the jealous manager in the office next door, but luckily he's out right now or he would certainly hear you, what with the thrusting and the groaning, you can even put your hand over her mouth, if it'll be better that way. Really, it's all right, most women appreciate a little submissiveness during sex, even if they moan, and this way she could just moan into your hand, and even the woman who was lying in wait for you on the shelf would start to get off now, overcome by the granditudiness of your thrusting, she wouldn't be able to help herself. Of course the whole time she would be thinking of you and what it would be like if your prong were inside of her, instead of that one there, and she knows that it would be magnificent because the two of you

once had a fleeting encounter, and she stroked your hammer and let you bang her to the bone, and even though it turned out not to lead to nesting, it was so sweet that she wants to get it on with you again, this time without shame, and she might die of longing, nesting be damned, if you fail to notice her as you survey the room, since banging archivists is a bit routine at this point, and that would be something new and get you hot to trot again, like the archive lady did a while ago, when she was still brand new and untested.

Now, suddenly, the woman on the shelf realizes that, whatever it takes, she needs to wrap the lips of her sticker-inner around the part of you that she was ready to lop off just a few minutes earlier, and she'd even like to lick a bit of sweat off of that tool, though not until after you've washed the archivist off inside of her. In her now nearly unspeakably swollen genitals, puffed up like an eiderdown pillow, and it may not be visible through the vegetation, but her face is wracked with pain. The next thing you know you're inside her, the new one, leaving the archivist startled to find that where before she was full, now there is only spread-open space. But immediately she spots the two of you, and gathering up her threads from the ground, she looks on in envy.

The woman the man was inside of before is hot and horny, lickety-split, to hell with inhibitions, she wants it now, and no fooling around. She has nothing to lose anymore, the freshness is out the window, but still, what the situation lacks in novelty it makes up for in pervishness, and being inside the woman

with castration desire, reduced to nothing but the longing to have her cunt pounded like a buffalo hide, the pleasure was even greater than it had been in the archivist's ass. Bursting prick whipping this way and that like a bitch flinging its pup around, his thoughts lost in fog, he humped his new mate like a marsh nymph he had hunted down out on the moors and now he was unabashedly going to have his way with her, and fast, since uh-oh, this isn't going to last long.

Especially once he feels the archivist's finger slowly creep between his cheeks and up toward his rectum, and the archivist's bush, all soaked with tears because he isn't banging her, the one he started out with, slides wetly up and down his thigh from behind, like a fresh little slut writhing on a pole at a strip club.

In short, all three of the guests in our little division of the Academy of Sciences' Institute of Oriental Languages want to get their rocks off good, and we aren't going to end the scene here. They'll just keep getting agonizingly closer and closer, but never actually get there, like two parallel lines that intersect at infinity, but in this case there are three, and everyone can choose the hero they erotically identify with the most and draw the line out for themselves.

TV Episode Three: Calories

I can also easily invite an additional sticker-inner to my plastic three-room suite. There is a second woman I keep in reserve for just such tender moments, and it's proven to be quite useful. Often the hammers aren't interested in splashing around in two pools per se so much as they simply enjoy seeing two hot babes nuzzle up to each other and spread their slipper-inners, so they can snuffle around and blow on them and lap their little tongues in circles all around the pielashes, and the clients want them to enjoy it tremendously too, since otherwise it's nothing but fulfilling the job requirements, and without at least a little shred of credibility, audiences tend to rate a performance dull.

After all, the reason clients come to my molded plastic three-room suite is to get a bit of humanity, not to sit there and click through some e-recording tossed to them like frozen fish to a polar explorer's dog.

Men are actually highly sensitive to how they're treated, and who wouldn't be, and I'm not talking about male vanity, which I'm not even sure what that means exactly, probably just another female slander against males.

Why is the kingdom of plants and animals so cantankerous, with constant squabbles over too little sticking in and too much, or the lack of willingness to be willing, of which females accuse even men of the thrush family, who slip it in, then quick give the slip and don't even chip in on building the nest? My God, I have so many questions that soon my TV series is going to be as overstuffed with ideas as my billfold was before I used a credit card and people gave me change in small bills, and these ideas, which I'll soon have piled up in my head like shit on the heads of old statues in zones with a high pigeon density, I'm afraid no TV crew could ever crank fast enough to get all my ideas down on film. Because my mind spins faster than anything I know, including that purple pinwheel of mine in the window, or the bicycle I sometimes drag out of storage, so instead of a run before breakfast, I lean into the pedals, flying past the post office, a building with no address, a fountain with two benches, a grocery store and a large complex of housing for office workers, to the even larger edifice of the shopping mall, where there are also small

bistros and cute little cafés, and I've given myself permission for a distinctive solo espresso with one packet of sugar, since I speed like a demon the whole way there and back, and I certainly burn more calories than a teaspoon of ground coffee and a little tiny packet of sugar contain, because the rest is water and that doesn't have any calories, even when it's warm, which I've always found a bit odd, since it gives much more of a boost than ice water when it's cold, and a boost is just calories being burned, I tell myself every time. Now there's a nut for our TV series to crack. That one for sure deserves an episode of its own.

I get perplexed whenever I see one of those programs on TV about the countries where winters are really bad and the poor people don't have anything to drink except water. Because if heated water, which is probably even double-boiled to make sure it's bacteria-free for the kids, doesn't contain any more calories than ice water, then they aren't really doing themselves any good by heating it up, and the wood, which must have calories, because people eat it in times of famine, that's a proven fact, in that case the wood that's burned to heat the water, thereby adding no calories to it, is not only a waste of time and labor for the person who carries it, splits it and stokes the fire under the kettle with it, but needlessly results in the loss of any calories it contained, which no one is going to scoop from the ashes with a teaspoon, if for no other reason than that eating it would stain your mouth, so while the calories would be saved in the chopping block for

harder times, as it is they're squandered, which means it isn't only rich countries that squander their resources but poor ones too, except the TV debate shows don't talk about that anywhere nearly as often.

Coffee does have calories, but whether it's instant or freshly ground, they never write how much on the package, so I'm worried that maybe it's too much, or almost none, like hot water, which would really annoy me, since after such a long bike ride, I have the right to some calories, and if coffee is almost calorie-free, then I would immediately start ordering something else at the cute little bistro café, say, half a tiramisu, and eat the other half the next day. I'm sure I could arrange it with the waitstaff somehow to stash it away for me. That way I wouldn't have to order some other new ridiculous dessert again the next day, since the bistro would have my half-eaten pastry specially waiting for me in the fridge, wouldn't that be nice, almost like one of those small towns where people still talk to each other, instead of just granting the wishes of each other's tools and sticker-inners, which is just servicing the machine to keep it in good condition, but rarely true romance, and as I said, I'm the traditional type.

I pick up the second woman on my bike. No moped or motorized scooter, nothing like that. It usually has nothing to do with my morning ride either. Morning clients tend to be the exception, so on those days I have to lug my bike up the stairs twice, but that only makes me feel better about my

flexibility. The mall is a popular meeting point for people who like to spend some time browsing around for a little something before they get together with friends, that way they kill two birds with one stone, and plus the displays are mostly mirrors with a few items added to fill them in, and when you want to look good for a date, it's nice to be able to double-check your hair and makeup beforehand, and the mirrors in the mall always reflect perfectly and are always ready to use, like a properly greased sticker-inner during working hours, and I can see the glistening as I clip his hairpiece with trimming scissors, squeezing a compact mirror between my knees, and at the center of the glistening and the wrinkles is a hole like a Cyclops eye. It isn't just the hammer that has a little eye, you see, the sticker-inner looks out at the world as well, and from the vantage point of a much larger superciliary arch. Only when I spread my thighs, though, since otherwise the eye is shut with a lid in a thin line that smiles good-naturedly when the sticker-inner gets off his shift and he's got a free weekend ahead of him, which he richly deserves.

When I arrive at the shopping mall early, and I'm waiting for the second woman, I look at the shop displays with my own eyes, not the Cyclops's, though, since the sticker-inner couldn't care less about my purchases, being an exemplary model of consumer restraint, unimpressed by even the most exclusive, fashionable brands, which in the shopping mall are available right at your fingertips, and when you have their

labels on your clothes, it's a surefire bet you'll have smooth sailing with everyone you meet.

Even so, being well dressed is something best done in moderation and always depending on the occasion, since a flawless appearance can also end up being counterproductive.

For my appointment with the second woman, for instance, I dress totally casually, seeing as we're both experienced professionals and any effort to improve your appearance for someone who already knows you only makes you look like a conceited hypocrite, or else like you have a guilty conscience.

To be clear, when I talk about the fine threads I replace on my regular shopping trips, I don't mean some flouncy miniskirt and black fishnet stockings that stink of pussy even after you pull them out of the washing machine, because some men like to use them as a gag, and if they aren't stuffing them in a woman's Cyclops eye, they're using them to stop up her mouth or tie her hands to the bars of the bed frame.

I can already hear the creak of the wires beneath the mattress, because the only reason films use the sound of wires groaning is to send a surge of blood to the audience's hammers and sticker-inners, which helps keep them from getting bored, and since e-films are the only e-things I really like, it sends a rush of blood to my slightly brainwashed brain too, just like everyone else's.

I also think it's done a bit of a number on the heads of the men who want to do me in tandem with another woman.

You can tell right away those are actors in those three-somes you see on a French bed, forming geometric figures

and performing acrobatics, and the director is yelling at them "to the right" and "down" and "shake that ass," since the results are so stilted that sometimes my sticker-inner splutters with laughter into my seat, even if the other people around me look hypnotized and in the dark of the theater probably can't tell who the prankster is, sitting there blowing raspberries, and that was how I actually found out for the first time that I know more about these things than most people, since I'm sure they were genuinely aroused by the threesome on screen, whereas I would have had to fake it, only why would I do that in a movie theater when I get enough of it in the course of a workday and I usually go to the movies alone, not with a man all my very own, for whom I would happily fake a groan of ecstasy if it pleased him, and it might, even if he knew it was just kidding on my part, since normally none of the films in multiplex distribution turn me on.

It wouldn't be the first time the two of us had gone out on the town after dinner in one of the mall's more than dozen restaurants in order to take a break from thinking, which I sorely need, given the constant stream of questions that intrigue me about the world, whereas the TV mystery series hasn't even begun shooting yet, so I need to give the clapper loader, sound designer, sound engineer and director, who towers over us all on his rolling stool, a bit of a chance to catch up by spending at least two hours in the dark of the theater, where I can't come up with anything decent, though lame sex scenes are when I'm most likely to switch off and slip back

into my thinking like a hand into a glove, even if it isn't always that comfortable, since given my uneducated smarts, I darn and mend my knee socks and, sure, I can make toes, but I still can't see with my head in the clouds, and figuring anything out when I'm in that state of mind is like trying to force a little boy to cum when he's old enough to shoot his spunk but doesn't know how. And not only do I not have that many answers, but I'm not even sure that I could explain to the director, so unapproachably stern-looking, perched high up on his stool, all the questions I have bored right through my head like an apple left long unattended, since no one has time for such a trivial fruit in the e-era, and if they do, then better a fresh one than a wormy one, and tout de suite it ends up in the trash, like so many other obviously defective and harmful things, but also the proverbial babies thrown out with the bathwater, and sometimes that's where my questions end up when the second woman arrives, and by this point I've been waiting out in front of the mall a good long while and I have to take the whole tub of half-baked ideas and dump it out, because we're on our way to a gig and I want to make sure I run smooth as a Swiss watch once we're there, so I can get myself back here, to the mall, on my own again, ASAP, and find peace on the concourse heaped high with enticing things, since at least they can maintain my attention long enough to keep my mind from wandering and getting hung up on nonsense.

But not everything I think of outside of working hours is nonsense. For instance, having the second woman ride on my

crossbar from the shopping mall to my house, while I pedal the whole way, to firm up my belly a little even before our joint appearance. That's my idea, and a good one, not only for my health, but also because it saves the second woman the effort, given that she clearly has no need to slim down or firm up, and anyone who points at us and shakes his head, as in, Look at those women horsing around like that, and at their age, I would say is traditional in the worst sense of the word, the type of tight-assed grouch even I, a self-professed traditionalist, try to avoid, and it doesn't take that much effort. That's just the kind of person I am, I'm one of those who doesn't even have to try that hard not to get indignant over people who need nothing more than a set of good tubeless tires to be cheerful. Though in many ways I'm just as crotchety as the grumpy majority of my neighbors, I also know how to take pleasure in life, and nobody's going to take that away from me on a bike ride back to my three-room flat. The wind ruffles our hair, making bright strips of highlights, which of course you can have done, there's a hairdresser in the mall too, but a highlight from the sun will never grow out and it doesn't go away until we reach the darkness of the shade in front of our building. It simply goes out like a light, though a few bleachlets may remain, because why else would my hair be a halftone lighter all summer than in winter, unless it's from those rides along the water in the sun?

I haven't been to the actual sea since I can't even remember, whereas the second woman goes fairly often with tubby clients,

servicing them on the beach and in the hotel room, but that isn't what I call vacation, just the thought of being employed twenty-four hours a day makes the skin in my sticker-inner crawl, all the way up and down his length and right up to his Cyclops eye. He would rail me with a rod for saying so, if he knew how, but now it's the rod that's going to rail him, because the client is already standing expectantly out in front of our building and his rod is about to start swelling soon, at least I hope, and there isn't much doubt, since it's extremely rare for the ones who request two not to have a couple under their belt already, they know their way around.

I could just as easily call the second woman TJ, Sylvia, or Miss Kolínská, but I like saying second woman, and the first woman is me, because the fuckshop where it takes place is mine, and I get the majority cut, just in case something were to happen to the furniture, or a glass were to break, it's only logical, sometimes the client will bring in some nice wine and the three of us will drink a toast, but that's as far as it goes, I don't drink on duty, as the police detectives say, who are all sharp dressers and also come to see us sometimes, but I promised to keep my mouth shut about that.

TV Episode Four:
Backwater Cyclists

We can already see him from here, standing in the distance. Our client. Stuffed into his pants like sausage, but it isn't enough to spoil our ride or our sunny mood. It's getting pretty boring anyway, what with the second woman going on about her seaside vacation, which was actually no vacation at all and she knows it, since she only had one day off a week. Cash in hand and off we go. At the sight of the fat cat, my sticker-inner swallowed drily, like a speaker before a speech, or at least that was my impression, sitting on the bike with the seat beneath my rear end, there's no way to tell exactly what he's mumbling down there. But he'll come

round, no doubt, and some cream will help him not to think about himself so much.

The thought that people travel so they can feel younger crosses my mind before I dismount and the second woman and I shake hands with the client, since if you travel by train or bus, there's always another new horizon popping up to surprise you, just one after the other, the way life comes at you when you're seventeen or twenty-two and still in a youthful frame of mind. I also often feel that way when I ride my bike, but as soon as I dismounted in front of that fat cat, the feeling totally left me and I could see my thirty everywhere, even if the only place it was actually written was on the address of my building and that's all.

Just a few moments ago, hair blowing in the wind, my age could go fuck a dog. Wind, like travel, is a rejuvenator. Riding against the wind smooths out your face better than any cream or the older ladies' trend of walking around with a portable blower to blow back their chubby, sagging cheeks and give their hair that carefree look. For some reason the fluttering movement gives that impression, it's a surefire unpatented idea, and battery makers would love it too, since it would run on four double-As, and they could also pack other ladies' accessories in along with it, like an epilator and a hair dryer with curling iron, the way they did with those massive five-story Swiss Army knives that bloated up from sucking in all those little tools that used to be separate, and now they weigh so much that they tear right through your pocket.

A ladies' portable blower wouldn't be that greedy, though, since for ladies of a certain age to lug around a blower with extensive accessories, on top of their blouse-stuffed handbag of menopausal first aid, would impede the unencumbered men in running the city. On every street corner you'd find some woman turned to face the building's façade, taking a break to change her blouse, while some other woman, on her way in to an important meeting, would be blowing air over her face in front of the building where her meeting was scheduled, since the blower's main drawback would be that any wrinkles you smoothed away would set back in again after just a few minutes, so you'd have to keep blowing your face all day, with just short breaks for work, and the female population's performance would drastically decline, and even more time would be lost moistening the skin, since the stream of air would deplete their skin of moisture, and with all that going on, the whole city would be paralyzed as a result of the ladies' meticulous self-preening, until finally it reached the point where the men would start to grumble that they would rather have them old and ugly than constantly preoccupied and blocking traffic, and I bet plenty of gullible women would fall for it, but my guess is that their sticker-inners wouldn't be rewarded with more frequent visits in return for their obedience.

When our fat cat client instructed me to bring a second woman for our next yee-haw, he was also particular about stipulating the age range. And then of course there are the special cases. Assuming they aren't violent or request that violence

be used against them, they usually have a deficiency of judgment regarding the age of the sticker-inner's owner, or, shall we say, the tender young sticker-inner's tender young owner, since that's the group these special cases have their sights set on, the ones with no more down than a freshly hatched chick, except that unlike the damp tufts on a baby chicken, the fuzzy down on these little girls with rare exceptions is dry as hell and there's no way to do it with them without lubrication, since they're about as interested in planting the alley, as the second woman calls hammering, as they are in math class, except if they don't go to class, their daddykins gives them a spanking, whereas big uncle-daddykins who ordered them for the fuckshop will give them a spanking just for walking in the door, since where else in the city is he going to find them, assuming he isn't the other kind of special case, who snatches little girls off the street to pummel them off in the bushes somewhere, but now we've stepped out of the realm of sexual services covered by rules and plunged feet first into the underworld of crime, albeit unorganized.

If anything like this were to happen in my neighborhood, I would firmly inform the gentleman from the police, whom otherwise I consider to be one of my favorite clients, that I refuse to satiate his fair-minded and exemplary pecker until the police solve the case and toss the assailant behind bars.

Then again, once they did solve the case, I would happily offer the gentleman from the police two anals free of charge, which normally, as he knows, I do only grudgingly and for an

outrageously exorbitant price, which is enough to discourage most clients, although for those few who say they wouldn't enjoy it nearly as much without the sacrifice of that stack of hard-earned cash, for that much money I grease up my ass and bend over, be my guest.

For some men in fact the paying is what turns them on the most, but most prefer not to. People talk about men as if they all belonged to the same family, when they don't even have a common stance on something so basic as finances. My advice to all those psychologistesses who go on about male vanity, men's unwillingness to be willing and their prioritizing watching TV over fine-tuning their relation-ship, which amounts to the women analyzing how it is that communication between them could break down so badly when they try so hard to make everything work and dabbing at their eyes with a handkerchief the whole time, looking to extort an apology for every little injustice, is that instead of greasing the wheels of family harmony, they should be greasing their sticker-inners and don't spare the cream on that pastry, since whatever differences there may be between my clients, men like to eat and screw, and constantly explaining that you aren't thin enough or that you have a headache that evening is the best way to launch them out of the family nest into the orbit of chronically late homecomings, which may mean yes, he's frequenting a fuckshop, and the little lady cries over spilled milk.

I do chat with the men sometimes, but I'm strictly opposed to any attempts at therapy. In my opinion the psychologist-esses would do best to keep their traps shut more often and devote their energy to the kitchen or the office or collecting trilobites, and just accept things as they are.

I don't claim that it's always possible. For instance, the wife of the fat cat who is studying me and the second woman right now as we nibble at each other's nipples in an attempt to heighten his orgasm, since his bangstick is one of the lazier ones, would probably bawl her eyes out if she saw what was going on, and come in to work the next day with her nose red as a beet. But, I'm sorry, that doesn't fall under my jurisdiction and it isn't my responsibility, because everyone here is over eighteen, and I say that because when it comes to the barely downy little girls the clients sometimes request, I feel a huge burden of responsibility, and I would jump down the throat of any man, no matter how elegant, who asked me for the number of a service for underage girls.

As a result of the responsibility I feel toward the young, I have a constant need to rejuvenate myself. In part to keep the flow of funds to my embossed credit card from being in-terrupted, and in part because a fresh-looking thirty-year-old can help dampen the lecherous desire for a fourteen-year-old. By taking care of myself, I help protect the young gals from premature insertion, although truth be told, most of the men who throng to the child fuckshops don't even know mine exists, and not even the most supple thirty-year-old pussy, a

master actress with all the aces up her sleeve, can convincingly play a fourteen-year-old.

To make it work requires a client who is at least halfway principled and finds my act of deception entertaining, so that while he fantasizes unlawfully, the hammering keeps him as hard as my ass, which he pumps full steam ahead, and we both get to tell ourselves that our little production is helping a girl on the other side of town prolong the phase of cute experimentation, whose most daring feat consists of a failed attempt to French kiss the boy from the classroom across the hall, which later that evening she'll recount in whispered tones into the ear of her stuffed teddy bear. In other words, I do my level best for my ass-shaking child rescue campaign to be more than just a bombastic boast that doesn't add up to diddly, since what the eye can't see won't hurt a flea, but for it to have genuine impact, the kind of rescue that makes a St. Bernard, trudging through the snowdrifts all day long with a barrel of rum around his neck to resuscitate reckless cross-country skiers buried under an avalanche, look like a puppy on a convalescent stroll after cardiological surgery. Bike rides aren't shit.

Look at the grannies in headscarves, riding boneshakers left and right in even the tiniest, most out-of-the-way Czech villages. Over the course of a lifetime, these backwater cyclists pedal more miles than any city slicker in an aerodynamic outfit on his tricked-out mountain bike could ever dream of, and what's more, they do it with bags of groceries dangling from

the handlebars and baskets full of pears and jars of raspberry jam, and yet they don't look like they're in shape at all, or any younger than their years, most of them. This is something to consider as another juicy topic for our TV mystery series, and I must say, it gives me a good feeling to devote my energy to something like this so systematically, but as far as arriving at an effective method for approximating the look of a fourteen-year-old, in order to spare her from the clutches of a nasty uncle-daddykins, it isn't going to help, even if we were to borrow a few original boneshakers from the technical museum to use in our series.

It isn't going to help, because even if no one can take away those women's title for number of miles pedaled, they still look more like they broke the record for eating those jars of raspberry jam that they chauffeur around in their baskets.

Neither biking nor any other calisthenics is going to save you, in and of themselves, that's the bottom line. Any woman who wants to look hammerable, and that's all of them, can't get by without maintenance. Whether or not your goal is as challenging and socially beneficial as pretending to be fourteen is beside the point.

So we've ended up in the same place I've landed every time so far. At the end of my wits, with the time-tested combination of pigtails, dimples, schoolgirl uniform with short skirt and knee socks, and above all, smooth-shaved runway, period.

That was exactly what the fat cat waiting for me and the second woman in front of the building that sunny day wanted,

and we made the transformation to fourteen right there in front of him, since he wanted to witness the process of transformation, and why not?

In the Biology Lab

Usually, I've got my look cooked up ahead of time, in line with the client's instructions, either that or the universal, yes, boring, high-heeled boots, stiff lace push-up bra, and tight-fitting blouse with tits spilling out, then I just flop down on the couch and flip through the channels or browse some light reading, and wait till the bell rings to give my lips a quick smear of red and check my eye shadow and mascara. Usually, I'm already stimulated in advance, so it all runs smoothly and right off the bat they can tell I'm a professional, which is why men pay a premium to come up to my flat, instead of shagging some tart off the street who stinks up the car with cheap cigarettes,

spouts foul language even if the customer didn't request it, then grabs the cash as soon as you're done and stuffs it in her rubber boots.

My clients have got class, and they pay for it happily, so even the most appalling ones are merely little cherries on the cake of the whore-fucking riffraff, and I try to offer a sweet taste of cherry in return, starting with pinpoint precision the moment the client rings the bell as I set my face to smile, all ready to go in my pussygear, freshly laundered and without so much as a speck of semen, which the roadside floozies always have on their boots and sometimes even in front, on their jeans skirt zipper.

You'll see, slow down the next time you drive by and check it out, they've got no class, those girls, or maybe it's just a lack of finances. Even the ones who give their outfits a quick washing-up in the sink, the semen is soaked in so deep they can't get the cumstains out of the fabric, it's just gross.

What I wanted to say, though, was our lack of preparation for the fat cat waiting out in front of the building was intentional on our part, since spying on our fourteenification was on his list as one of the things that gets him hot to trot quick as a wink, and even if it hadn't been, when a client requests an outer sticker-inner smooth as a little girl's, I wait to shave it until the absolute last minute, when the man is more or less standing in the doorway, because my bush grows nonstop, just like I age, which is to say twenty-four hours a day, and not only does it show more than aging, but even worse, it

feels to the touch, because from the minute I finish shearing my sandpapery outer cunt, feebly disguising it as a phony fourteen-year-old's, I slowly begin to rethirtify, and any client who wanted a little girl but chose me instead, whether out of fear, principle, or goodwill, isn't the type to be interested in a regular fetching thirty-year-old.

In short, we tried to convince the fat cat that we were little girls, in every way we could. As we pulled on our skirts, he pulled down his pants, and when we zipped up and he zipped down in perfect synchronization, the second woman and I would give each other a wink. It was an Oscar-worthy performance, and the fat cats with experience appreciated it too.

I wouldn't say, the way some men do, when we get to talking, before or after, on some totally unrelated subject, that my work is my hobby. It's more that feeling of satisfaction when a job goes like clockwork. I know what that's like, and with the fat cat it went like clockwork right from the start, a joy to behold. By that I don't mean that he came in sixty seconds and left me and the second woman in peace to chat for the rest of the hour while he took a bath to put himself in the mood to go back home. No. By that I mean that we ran our act and his hammer ran along with us, jumping right on our wavelength, bobbing her little head up and down, and the fat cat didn't even have to engage in manual mode.

The second woman and I played frisky little schoolgirls who are accidentally locked in the biology lab and, over the course

of a long night, come to know each other intimately. When we came up with the idea, and we even had an appointment to talk it over in my favorite bistro at the mall, the second woman suggested it not be an accident that we get locked in but a prank on the part of the biology teacher, who I don't know why but the second woman started calling Griswold, and who decides to keep the girls trapped in there overnight, so he can help them explore their newly blossoming bodies and at the same time give his spirits a bit of a lift, though of course only as an afterthought.

The way the second woman imagined it, Griswold was actually sort of a guide to the girls, a sort of older buddy-brother, so the girls didn't have to worry about whether or not it was alright to yank his doodle, which with all their clumsy rubbing and tugging would then start to rise, eliciting genuine astonishment from the girls at the sudden hugeness of the goings-on beneath the teacher's belly, and this astonishment would warm the kind-hearted Griswold in all the right places, culminating in the tearing of hymens at the end of the night. An even bigger surprise was the fact that their little Cyclops eye was so deep that his whole huge dandy could slip in there all in a single whoops, and there would be a little ouch but soon the girls would be happily purring away, and then moaning, and then coming like the whores in the fat cat's fantasies, which he knows as well as we do are misguided, no whore comes at the same time as her clients, but that's what we pretend, and why not, if the client likes it. Just so long as he doesn't mind

when he sees me rubbing lube in my sticker-inner during the break, so he knows I'm not really getting turned on and otherwise I'd be as dry as tinder, but most clients don't care if I oil up and some even like to help.

But we ended up dumping the idea of Griswold, since who was going to play him? The fat cat pays to have a good time, not to memorize lines. Then we weren't sure if having a narrator instead of Griswold would be sexy enough, so in the end we just dropped the whole thing. The story wasn't really that developed anyway, so we agreed that we would just improvise, depending on the client.

It wasn't that we were too lazy to rehearse or rack our brains, as I'm sure some smart alecks out there think, assuming women for hire are stupid, but more a question of our willingness to adapt. After all, that's what we're paid for: to fulfill the client's wishes, not to teach him the part of Griswold, which would have been fulfilling ours. Because if the fat cat doesn't feel comfortable in his role as well as turned on by the scenario, which is the usual combination men prefer, then the fact that we thought up the whole thing for his sake isn't going to move him or his hammer, since hammers by nature are skeptical of any explanation.

So in the end the scenery for the biology lab was very loose and more or less just for the sake of us two. I put the cage with my little molded-plastic yellow bird from China on the table by the bed, along with the scale from my kitchen counter, even though the second woman objected, and she was

probably right, that a scale's more the type of thing you would expect to see in a physics lab, and it wouldn't be the same one you use for flour and shelled nuts, but I put it there anyway, and the second woman added a little stuffed bunny that she leaned against the wall, which she dug out of her handbag in a moment of sheer inspiration. A lot of cunts carry talismans like that around in their bags with their lubricants, tampons, and lipstick, which whatever but I don't get. She ended up taking the rabbit back when the fat cat made a face. That's the way it goes. Men aren't into stuffed animals.

As he rammed his overcooked soft-shell lobster in between us, we dipped our fingers into our sticker-inners and drew sticky patterns on each other's bellies. By that point we weren't wearing our T-shirts anymore, but we still had on our skirts and knee socks, and our pigtails and pert little noses freckled with magic marker. It's a shame there isn't any way to simulate an upturned nose without a ridiculous investment in plastic surgery, because, if I may, a nose like that on a teenage girl is just the cutest thing. Still, the fat cat moved pretty quickly from cute to fuckfest. Once he saw me licking the second woman and heard her sighs he couldn't hold back. She was a brilliant sigher, and believe it or not, I actually did get a teeny tad wet, since after all we were pretty good friends, she wasn't just a fuckstomer, and that feather-light wave of unfeigned arousal may have been just the thing that got the fat cat's motor running, since, as I said, he was no beginner, but had

a finely developed sense for authenticity, like all my regular customers, who at a certain point understandably are fed up with fake panting, and a play-acted, bed-rattling, eyeball-rolling gasp can't hold a candle to even the slightest hint of genuine arousal in a paid-for whore.

He nailed the second woman first, probably because she had been exposed to his admiring gaze for so long already and was still glistening from my licking, then he did me from behind and then jizzed on the pillow and there was at least a soupspoon full.

It was a good day all around, from start to finish.

After the fat cat, we had a very unsophisticated client, who only wanted the two of us to act out a little comedy sucking each other's breasts, then he gave me a little hammering and came inside the second woman, and the last client of the day, I always try to schedule all the ones who want two for the same day, so the second woman doesn't have to commute all the way across town, here and back, just for one customer, so the last client was a total beginner, which was a little unusual. He got carried away by the fact that he was getting double treatment, and after just a minute of fellatio, abruptly creamed in my mouth while the second woman was sliding her tongue in and out of his butt cheeks.

Leaning his arms against my wardrobe, his legs shook like a miniature pinscher's. Which I must say, I wasn't expecting. It was supposed to be just for starters, a standard warm-up, so to speak, but before I could say hold your horses, which

with my mouth full of his erection was obviously impossible, he got off and the two of us punched out.

The quick finisher was also the youngest of all our clients that day, and there weren't too many young ones on other days either.

He was nineteen at most, and to judge from his suit, he came from a very good family. Sometimes fathers even bring their own sons in with them. Instead of a trip to some coconut-covered island in the Pacific to toughen them up, they treat their son to an evening in here, and afterward they go out together, just the two of them, man to man, for a drink and a levelheaded discussion. How else is a father supposed to let his son know that he's truly grown-up and from now on they're equals, instead of one obeying the other? My own personal theory is, if they can fool around together with whores, then the tiresome inequality of the parent-child relationship can be stripped away like my brassiere, which was all that this young lad could manage before his legs began to shake, laying the ground for a new phase in the father-son relationship.

Life is portioned up like that into pieces, like an orange or a cake, the only difference being, they often aren't tasty little nuggets but big chunks of time, years even, that are hard to swallow, though I confess I don't know much about it. Let others be unhappy, if those are the stories they want to write. Everything I know about the complications of childhood, growing up and all those other juicy bits, comes entirely from light reading.

TV Episode Five:
Who Made a Mess of the e-World?

As for my light reading, I sometimes sit down with it when there's nothing appealing on the channels and I'm expecting a client to ring in just a bit. When I'm just in maintenance mode, since I don't want to drop anything on myself at the last minute or spill anything on the floor, I reach for a book, and some of them, it turns out, talk about the mishaps of growing into manhood, which, again, confirms for me what I've already thought for a long time, and that's that our world is too e- and not enough human, and it isn't just because the voice that answers on the other end of the phone is more and more often a machine instead of a person, and a machine with

no intonation announces the station stops at train stations, and the voice on a mobile phone that says to leave a message is also often the mailbox instead of the owner, saying, This is Koudelka, or Příbramský, or whoever.

Also usually when a client of mine has his phone ring over at my place, he's got it set to go straight to his mailbox, so visits to whores must be on the increase if you're getting people's mailbox voices more often nowadays. I don't know who's responsible for making such a mess of it all, and by now maybe you suspect that you're standing at the birth of the latest topic for our TV mystery series, which has the potential to solve every puzzle that currently baffles us. I always get fired up like this when I start in on anything e-, since the planet is so overcrowded with e-stuff it must be falling off by now, though I realize, so you can see for yourself not every cunt's a dimwit, that there's no such thing as earthly gravity outside of Earth, so however much the Earth has to carry on its back, nothing can knock it down or snap its neck, and at worst all the little thingies will circle around in orbit with a lack of oxygen, hopping and skipping around and bumping into each other, but they won't fall down anywhere.

Of course, this is just further incentive for all the e-companies to keep churning out more and more e-crap unchecked, since as long as nobody puts their foot down and says this has gone far enough, most people and companies will just go right on spewing all of their nonsense and e-products left and right without a second thought, the same way the client

does with his sperm in my plastic three-room flat. Having the plastic is practical when it comes to that, actually, you just wipe it all off with a damp cloth and rinse out the cloth afterward.

I always get worked up like this about the whole world, even when I was just planning to talk about one thing, and on a totally different subject. That's because I'm an intuitive type and easily get carried away, but then again, you can trust me to say what I feel and say nothing when I feel nothing, or the opposite, when I feel too much for words to be able to contain. But the one thing I just can't get to the bottom of, no matter how I try, is what crossed my mind when that shaky young gentleman pinscher left and I was thinking how much my credit card would enjoy drawing from his dad's account, as opposed to that young pup's piggy bank, and then how the way fathers trained their sons with whores, in this case me and the second woman, was such a human and, in the e-world, infrequent phenomenon, because the light reading that I used to kill time while waiting for my clients said that young men on tropical islands in the South Pacific also had to undergo rites of passage. Initiation into things they didn't know, and they probably also didn't go so well the first time, but otherwise the young pups wouldn't be accepted among the grown men, and I think we here could learn a thing or two from them. I don't know exactly what the connection is, but the more things are e-, the more men are sissies, and by that I don't mean that they carry around a man bag, with deodorant

spray for bad breath and roll-on for their armpits, I like that kind of thing, but that instead of seeking relief naturally, with their hammer in a pussy, an ever increasing number are special cases, and not just the violent types or the ones who have to be addressed as a shit-eating shithead and don't get hard till their ass is whipped to shit and their cheeks are striped with welts, but the ones who still long for cuddle-wuddles from their mommie-wommie, and sometimes they want to be punished too, but mollycoddled along with it, like a runny-nosed little kid with his mommy kissing his scraped knee, and they're the ones who imagine me as a mommy-cum-psychotherapist, and I do that too, as long as there isn't too much of it, but I think to myself, I wonder how many e-devices you wipe with an antistatic duster each week, you family man asshole with milk dribbling down your chin, and you still want to slurp from my tits, even if no doubt you're a model father and husband at home and a hushabye teddy bear at night, depositing bland trickles of sperm at weekly intervals into your wife, who thinks it's normal to call a repairman to hammer in a nail and that an orgasm means when people just keep hammering the same bottom over and over again, namely, you hers, with her in a cute little black negligee and the lamp on the nightstand switched on, and that that's what it means to be a proper grown-up couple and have a healthy sex life, with nothing getting drooled on and the hubby snoring soon afterward. But every mumsyfucker is different. Not all of them are just bored little tykes who don't know how to ask for anal

at home and feel overly confined in their cozy little love nest. In fact, usually they're just ordinary poor slobs, and for the right price I'll serve myself up, so that there in the relatively dramatic setting of my fuckshop, in exchange for their hard-earned money, with more or less basically solid justification, which I couldn't care less about, they can squirt their loads in freedom, whereas the rest of their life runs like clockwork and it's just occasionally a tad on the humdrum side.

The true mumsyfuckers have enough of that little drama at home, and the fuckshop, a quiet backwater of kissed knees, offers a gulf of solace, because what an orgasm means to these men's wives was drilled into their heads by all those sex scene disasters you see at the multiplex, which whenever they happen my sticker-inner farts with laughter into my seat, and I would only be willing to moan during them, as I said, for the enjoyment of a man all my very own, so that sitting there in the seat next to me, in the dark, he would get an urge to stroke himself, or maybe just enjoy my sighs, or maybe all of me, or, sigh, even love me.

The mumsyfuckers' wives who fancy themselves well informed and up to date know very well an orgasm isn't a lamp shining on a new negligee and fucking the same dick time and again, and torture the mumsyfuckers with their long lists of demands. All the top tips from the magazines for spicing up your sex life, spending hours searching for the G-spot like morons, having the hubby play Lumberjack Bill when in real life he gets faint just at the thought of killing a carp, but even

that isn't enough. To hell with conscious women, wives or not, in this case a ring on the finger means nothing, it only makes it that much more a pity, and these men want to be pitied, because with a wife it's for a lifetime, and conscious women want it all.

The tender games when their tummy aches and they have their period, the Kama Sutra positions with yoga breathing techniques, and keeping it up all night long with your pecker hard as granite and no going soggy in between acts, it's one scene after the next, because a woman deserves her money's worth too, no one can claim she doesn't have the same right to satisfaction as a hammer does at the end of a hectic day in the soulless e-city, and by the same token, just like back in cave days, a woman also has every right to sometimes get in the mood where she wants a man to give her a licking, to ram it in and slap her ass, and as long as he's being playful, maybe even call her a little slut while he's at it. There are also some truly special cases who are women, it isn't just men who are fertile ground for perversion in the e-age, but I'm not talking about that now.

I'm talking about the conscious wife of the mumsy-humper who comes pounding on the door of my molded plastic nook not because his wife didn't want to put out for him or wouldn't do it any way but missionary-style, but because she had too many wild ideas and different strokes for different folks, and when on top of that, according to the schedule magnetized to the fridge, he's expected to wipe out

the crapper on Tuesdays, Thursdays and Saturdays, attend family meetings every Monday, and every other night he has to play Lumberjack Bill, even though he has nothing in common with him except a hairy back, I don't blame him for sniveling, but I'm not here to serve as a marriage counseling service, and the second I hear any mumsydiddler sing that tune, it sets my teeth on edge. Usually, I still end up servicing most of them anyway, including a five-minute heart pouring-out, which always turns out to be the reason — along with the fact that in the fuckshop, unlike in their conjugal bedroom, they don't have to show anything — they came to see me in the first place, since their wife is a perfect female specimen and what more could they want?

Miss honeybundelusciousness?

TV Episode Six:
Which the Audience Will Never See

I don't know exactly why, and by now you know why I don't know is because I'm so intuitive, but I wouldn't do a family troubles episode for my TV mystery series, and I'd even go so far as to say that any conscious woman operating under the impression that she and I belonged to the same tribe and therefore I had personally demeaned her with my silly blather about family life, which I don't know shit about, since, and this is what she would say, I'm a tarty cunt who thinks being a high-class indoor whore instead of a curbside tramp somehow makes her more interesting or less deserving of public disgrace, although either way, that's just how I earn my

living, yes, from the two-timing of so many heads of families you could count them on the fingers of both hands and still not even come close, so if some conscious woman were to get an episode on family life, as I've heard it described by the mumsyfuckers, into the series over my objections, because she thinks she could do more justice to the material, since for a woman to be portrayed as sharing the guilt for her husband's two-timing would be an outrageous injustice as she sees it, if this woman were to succeed in getting the episode into the series, and it would be a fierce battle, since I would really be strongly opposed, though I doubt any feline maneuvers, such as face scratching with fingernails or spreading slanderous rumors, would come into play, this conscious woman, were she to succeed in spite of everything in having the episode run on the series and getting the material shot, although I don't think that would happen, since I don't mean to toot my own horn, but the director, the DP, the sound engineer, and the technical director, in short, everyone except the second assistant camera, who is the one who holds the clapper, would probably be men, since they make up the majority in the more important professions, but if, in spite of everything, she managed to get the material shot, in that case I would resort to shady feminine practices without any qualms whatsoever, and like the flexible comic-book heroine and crimefighter the Catwoman I would scale up the drainpipe into the film studio building, and, using a key borrowed from someone on the crew, you ask what they received in return and whether it was

my body, and maybe, it might be, yes, using the key I would unlock the editing room and find all the above-mentioned material that had been shot and was now waiting to be developed, and cut it up with a big pair of scissors, and as the pièce de résistance, I would slide back down the drainpipe, tiptoe unseen past the entrance gate, and ride the late-night connections back to my fuckshop as if nothing had happened. I would leave no proof whatsoever, and naturally, as the creator of the series, I would act utterly stunned and crestfallen on hearing the news of the break-in.

Why so many perilous adventures and activism, you ask, when up until now I looked like the kind of woman who walks home from work, in fact she doesn't even have to, since she's almost always home and at most goes out for a run in the morning, rides her bike down to the mall for an espresso, and spends some happy moments there, strolling among the heaps of items, credit card in hand? I'd like to see some of those uncle-daddykins clients looking to screw fourteen-and-unders in the slammer. Maybe if I didn't put out for the police detective unless he put one of them to rot behind bars, he's one of my most solvent customers, that might work, right? And all of a sudden I get the urge to break the law myself and commit theft, destruction of property, and trespassing. That's what they call a double standard, not seeing the beam in your own eye while you criticize the speck in your brother's, it's a quote from that famous old tome.

Of course, I didn't make up this stuff I'm rattling on about here. Either I experienced it myself, or somebody told me, or it comes from my light reading. It was a collection of real-life experiences, in fact, that taught me not to like people who are too smart. There's something e- about people like that. Or maybe they're just smartypants, but it isn't wise to wallow in psychological matters, especially given how closely tied they are to sticker-inners and hammers and their mutual coordination. It's certainly far more reckless than climbing a drainpipe at night and letting the editing technician bang me in return for loaning me the key. Because a broken leg heals in a splint after a month, but a hammer that's lost its confidence, you can't even raise it up with a jack, which is why men who can't cope with the demands of conscious women come to me in my fuckshop, instead of talking it over, as would seem logical, with their wives.

But any hammer that doesn't want to write itself off entirely knows that excessive talking is guaranteed to do just that. Which is why men who are married to conscious women go elsewhere when they need to restart their hammers, and then they can return to their conjugal calisthenics with greater confidence. It sure isn't going to happen at home.

At the fuckshop, though, the debacle comes included, and my cunt, unlike a wife, couldn't care less. Being subjected to analysis by a woman, even one in good faith, is the ultimate kiss of death to a hammer's well-being, and what else would that episode be but a bunch of talking psychology heads?

If I had a hammer and I had to be subjected to all of that, it would crawl back up in my belly and hide. All the demands and analyzing and playing the role of Lumberjack Bill, who can fuck *and* wash greasy saucepans *and* be emotionally sensitive, all rolled up into one great big do-it-all package. The whole thing is just too e- for me. I'm not e-, and neither is my sticker-inner, so I doubt that hammers are either.

I have little trust, if any, in anything that comes with wrenches and is "some assembly required," all the "versatile use" and "flexible design" you see in modern kitchens these days. I don't really go for that, yet so many people are knocking down walls and partitions to put them in, and the whole household is nothing but drilling and dirty dust, and it grates on the nerves of the neighbors too, since they can't use pots pressed up to the wall to eavesdrop anymore, and instead they're subjected to high-decibel jackhammers.

These kitchens aren't really even kitchens anymore, and the living rooms, which they connect with them to make it into one big room, are nonliving rooms joined to the nonkitchen that offers the woman preparing an instant meal constant oversight of the man while he engages in his favorite activities, such as reading the paper, watching the news, and scratching his crotch, visible at all times and ergo under fire by critical remarks, since women typically don't enjoy these things and don't really understand what makes them so appealing, especially not when they're right there and the two of them could be having a chat in their nonkitchen-slash-livingroom combo,

seeing as they sunk all that money into it, and the man wanted it too, after all, even helped with the renovations, the work-ers were Ukrainians, they all are nowadays, so why not take advantage of the new view of the couch from the cupboards for a mutual exchange of information and opinions about junior's report card and the new battery they need to order for the bathroom, but also a heart-to-heart to firm up their relationship, with a focused assessment of their shortcomings and joint obligations to work toward discontinuing them, why, the woman would be the first to commit to working even harder, and they could also give each other a blow-by-blow of their day, or otherwise, good golly, in a year and a day they might wind up complete and total strangers.

My molded plastic three-room suite has no kitchen-slash-livingroom, no woman preparing instant meals, and no man on the couch thinking who knows what, I won't even try to imagine. Where they might be and how many of them, in their coalliances, and how many times a week they bang, and whether they take a hard stand on that, or have hard feelings toward each other, or if the man ever gets hard anymore, since the woman hardly comes from behind the counter, and though it seems like things around there are hard enough as is, under the duvet at night it's barely hard at all, so as creator of the show I have the right to say scratch that when it comes to my TV mystery series. Because not only is it pretty boring and TV time is more expensive than ours, and I wouldn't even want to watch it on my own time, but I guess I'm also just sort of

the rescuing type, like a St. Bernard with a pacemaker, except that it's even more of a burden considering how responsible I feel for juveniles', and especially little girls', behinds, which should be protected against fuckage under penalty of death for any man who would jam his wormy gun into them even once, and the whole thing just came over me, along with a feeling of family happiness, even though I couldn't care less about either one, since I'll never be a little girl again, I don't have a girl or a family, and there isn't much chance that will change.

But still, I guess public affairs get me riled up, and if men are so worn out by their family life that their shiny peckers just dangle limply like sloth tails, then they won't be able to screw out enough police detectives to put the screws on the uncle-daddykins buggering our little girls. I can't help but see the two as connected, so maybe my rescue attempts make some sort of sense, and whether they do or not could be the seventh question for our TV series, though it is a bit egocentric as infotainment intended for a general audience.

I realize we all have our quirks, that most of us are born with flaws and the family environment often completes the work of destruction, so people can't be blamed for being who they are, but it seems like the e-world plays to the worst in us, and besides, assuming that's all true about our birth and upbringing, and the e-world governs our affairs, though it wasn't our idea and the ones who came before us are what forge us into who we are, then I don't know who or what's at fault, and the uncle-daddykins, the violent ones, and the ones

who can get off only if their ass is whipped to a bloody pulp are just mere products of circumstance, free of guilt for what they are. That's why I don't like it when clients try to turn my fuckshop into a therapist's office, because the bad guy, under the barrage of touching details about his ill-starred past, ends up looking like just another poor slob and the good guy like a lucky stroke of fate, born into a tidy little family with no deviations in finance and rare fluctuations in the bangers of his mama's ass.

The violent ones often had an uncle who liked to crawl under the duvet with a bloated udder poking from under his belly, just the right size for a child's mouth to drink from, so the little boys grew up angry at the world, and rightly so, because not everyone has such a disgusting creep for an uncle, and who the hell decided which family he would hatch into?

The ones who enjoy being kicked around and lashed with a whip often had some lovely person like that in the family, a harsh mommy, say, who spanked them for failing to clean their shoes properly, except in their case they aren't angry at the world, but at themselves, for sliding down the rope into it, since according to some, the unborn soul takes up residence in that little bundle of flesh and bone by its own decision, of its own choice, in which case it's your own fault if you grow up with a harsh mommy, you can't lay blame on anyone else, and the desire to be constantly punished for it is perversely justified by some teachings on volition of the self, and I'll stop right there or I might say something horrendous, and

tomorrow a piece of balcony might fall on my head, and I wouldn't be able to get my police detective to prove it was some smart aleck who dropped it on me, even if I didn't put out and didn't put out and didn't put out.

It isn't that being clever and analytical never lead anywhere, but, on the contrary, they lead to so many things at once, with arrows pointing every which way, like a signpost on a hiking trail, that all you can do is just stand there, shaking your head, or take a gamble and choose one more or less on blind faith, and that's why I gave up on smart aleckry. Just like on an actual hike, where I'll start out on the blue trail, then come to a junction with arrows pointing in every direction, none of which I'm familiar with, and make up my mind at random, choosing the route with the gentlest ascent that looks the least muddy, or else decide based on the name. Green Peak always loses out to Silver Saddle, and tough luck for Wolf Gorge going up against Wishing Well Camp.

Lucky for me there are uncle-daddykins, with their love for little girls, or sometimes I really wouldn't know whom to point the finger at, or that even in this e-day-and-age, with its unhealthy environment and sinister nursery school teachers, there are still just plain bad people, who can't blame anyone but themselves, not something or somewhere, no, no one but them.

Because the biggest whiners, the ones who try to make me their therapist, sometimes get me so wound up I'd just as soon sit and nod along to all their sob stories. But the movement

of my head, which at first was just my way of saying, Roll that little imp of yours back into your drawers and scram, started to eat at me after a while. I was beginning to sympathize with them against my will, and I could have done with a hobnail boot or a head to the wall myself, since once that happens I lose all judgment, and that also causes me problems at the mall, because suddenly every cute little sweater I lay eyes on looks appealing in one way yet offputting in another, so even if I have plenty of man milk on my credit card in the form of exchangable tokens, it's useless to me, so that's why, and that's also why it's a good thing we've got uncle-daddykins around.

Because when anger and indignation have constant doubts as to their own legitimacy, not only do they not go away, but their suppression causes them to give off a foul stink and turn sour, and suddenly one day you dump a bucket of shit on a totally innocent man, because your cup is overflowing and it has to get out, even if it doesn't go in the right place, like a man's spunk into another sticker-inner when his wife's has been out of order a long time for whatever reason, and now answer the question yourselves, without the help of the TV series, whether a hammer has the right to that or not.

Because I know I'm not suited to answer those kinds of questions, not that I feel guilty, no one's getting me to open that can of worms, let other people stir the pot of moral self-flagellation, but I mean given my profession and its tra-ditions, because I'm a pro, which is why you won't find any records about my clients from the police department lying

around my flat, or about the second woman, not even her initials, which means my molded plastic three-room suite could easily be that weird-looking flat with the stripped door and the lady you tell your children not to talk to or even pet her cat.

A Little Girl and
TV Episode Seven:
Women Worrying Their Pretty
Little Heads

Ah, children. Children and their uncle-daddykins, for whom there is no excuse in this world, and if there is a hell, then fwoop, down they all go, because this is no evil on a path marked by sketchy arrows that winds up with parents' excuse notes for unsightly conditions at home, no, this is evil that evils, which means now I'm going to tell you what I know from them, so that you can picture the eviling, and I'm going to warn you right from the start, you can swear on your heart all you want, but more likely you'll need your hand on your fly, so that nothing down there starts to rise, and be afraid, be very afraid, that it will.

On the other hand, to help us dispel the stress a little, I can't control my getting wet either, and just in case you're wondering whether it ever feels good having some grimy fat cat plow me till my molded-plastic yellow bird rattles in its cage like a motor scooter over the cobblestones, and whether I agonize over it after because there wasn't the slightest smidgen of emotional involvement, the answer is no, it doesn't give me a stomachache, and yes, one out of every few hundred does bring me to the Králický Sněžník of ecstasy with his hose pipe, and maybe one in eight thousand can take me to the summit of Nanga Parbat, so that's still yet to come, since I won't be banging my eight thousandth until just before I retire.

But the wettening that I can't control, which is what I had in mind, isn't the same as that and it's nothing to be ashamed of, either. But just as the paths of fate are inscrutable, my sticker-inner is the path of my destiny, partly by virtue of the fact that he provides for me, but also because he grows moist irrespective of any human touch, and I don't mean only climaxing against my hands, since obviously they're human too, or the damp after a long bicycle ride, but dripping at a vista of the sun setting over the landscape, bleeding red into a blackened sky filled with tattered clouds, yes, then too, but, unlike some bum's rod growing stiff as he waits for the school-girls to come squealing out the door at the sound of the bell, what I'm talking about is totally harmless and purely my own private affair, although with the clouds and the grassy sod all around and the magic light they may actually look a lot alike,

and if there were a little fawn grazing out in the meadow, a little bear romping about or some cheerful little bunny lolling in the grass, it would look even more alike. The softness of the shapes, both round and long at the same time, yet firm to the touch when you grip that delicate arm in your hand and there is no resistance, just boundless trust, or a slight touch of fear, which you can either dispel or let slowly grow and play with it like a little ball, and easily move those big eyes to fragrant little tears, which the pervert wipes away with a tender stroke of his hand as he gently takes the little girl onto his lap, and it becomes more and more tender from there. Her baby-fine hair, which smells so sweet, and now at last that they're alone he's no longer afraid someone will come and take her away from him. Her silky little back and buttocks, warm against his knees, and all the rest is fresh and ready, and he'll be the first to test it out, where on big women who've already blossomed it's worn shiny like old sleeves and their stretched-out pussies have lost their grip ages ago, so your hammer knocks around inside, whereas now it's going to be clenched in the tightest grip he's ever felt, and in return he's going to treat the little girl with the most attentive care, because he can feel her fragility as if it were his own, and soon he's going to merge with her and it won't be violent in any way, he'll just take that little girl with the firm little ass sitting on his knees and pull her onto his lap and ever so slowly run his hand up the inside of her thigh, and then slip a finger under the elastic on her stockings and run his hand a little bit further down, it's all

so close together, all the distances are so small that he could cover her whole tummy with his palm if he wanted, but now he's got his hand on her private parts, the little muffin, maybe what's what they call her at home, and his fingers' surprise at feeling her smoothness. He's been waiting so long he can barely wait, but he didn't know it would be so exciting he would get hard just from running his finger back and forth on her little slit, and he sinks it in a little deeper, and the little girl gives a yelp, but then falls quiet and stays that way. Just before that, though, she wiggles around a bit on his lap, and it feels tremendous, and he thinks if he settled her on his lap the right way, the pleasure would spread evenly all over his body, and he wraps his arms around her narrow waist and slides her back and on forth on his knees, running her up and down his cock, which now is fully gorged, back and forth, back and forth, and the little girl doesn't make a peep when he strips off her stockings and slips his finger back in her slit again, this time from behind, and it's tight and tiny as can be, and he gets even harder as he pushes his fingers in, one by one, then two, three at a time, and runs them lovingly in and out, in and out, and gets even harder, and then when she sits right down on his rod and both of them are naked, he lifts her up a little bit, light and docile, totally quiet, and his flushed rod looks for the best spot between her cheeks to thrust into her slit from behind, and meanwhile he sniffs at her baby-fine hair, which smells of dried meadow grass, and when he finally gets her lined up in the right position and

pulls her down on top of him, he's suddenly on the verge of coming and pulls up short.

It's been a long time since he was wedged inside of someone with a grip as tight as this, and his dick is practically drooling, but he manages to hold back, even when he presses his middle fingers down on the little girl's nipples and then circles them with his fingers and pinches them gently, they're just about to blossom, you can sense it's coming soon, but for now her breasts are still totally flat, and as he rubs them, at the same time thrusting into her faster and faster, he can't even feel the nipples under his fingers, and the last few thrusts he does standing up. Holding the little girl with both hands around her hips, fucking her, in and out, in and out, then jams her down deep on his shaft one last time.

He probably paid her a compliment, and it made her happy that he treated her like a little lady, talking nice and smiling at her, even though she got a C that day, it's nice when grown-ups don't make a big deal out of grades. It was a little odd at first, walking down the street holding hands with someone she didn't know, but she got used to it after a while, since she knew the street well and the shops on both sides had their lights on, with music coming out, and then they turned a few corners and went inside a house.

Fourteen-year-olds are duly informed in advance what to expect in a fuckshop specializing in uncle-daddykins, assuming it's a reputable establishment. The men just do them while

they lie there, well lubricated, chewing gum with a bored look on their face, and for some uncle-daddykins that indifference is actually what turns them on the most, which is odd, since when I look apathetic, the clients usually get pissed off and start cursing that they want a show for their money, and don't calm down until I start moaning and groaning and they get it up again, but there's something about an oblivious-looking girl chewing gum.

Maybe it's because the pervert would like to slam his fuck-stick into that little brain of hers and fuck the thoughts right out of it, just like he'd like to do to her flexible little ass, because who knows, maybe that little girl's brain is just as tight as her pussy and would be just as good a fuck.

When some apathetic miss high-and-mighty also has stiff tits, that's even better, since that means maybe she likes it and the whole thing's just a put-on to get her uncle-daddykins' motor revved. Why else would her tits be so damn stiff and her nipples all puffed up if she didn't want to lick all up and down his pecker and keep it in her sticker-inner as long as she can? The young missy just needs a little rearing is all, which you can give her by sliding your pecker all around her tits while she lies on her back staring off into space, and whatever it is she's dreaming about will be revealed when you cram your pole in her mouth and her eyes pop out of her head and her dreams go rolling across the floor like peas, which uncle-daddykins could pick up and throw against the wall and she wouldn't even react, which is why you have to teach her some more,

as he slaps that ass that will soon be gross, for now it's still prime, but it's good for the girl to be embarrassed, she won't be as impudent with him if she thinks that she's ugly, in which case it's practically a miracle the gentleman has any interest in her at all, and he can dig his trowel into her buxom cushions wherever he pleases, and tweak her tits, which are like balloons and not even a little deflated, but tight as a drum, since they've just grown in and may still grow another six to twelve months, and that's why they're so sensitive to the touch, hot and full of youth. Maybe there really is something to the superstition that virgin blood is healing, because on the way home this uncle-daddykins feels completely rejuvenated, much more so than if he had gone with his coworkers to that silly steambath, which he declined, and he did the right thing.

So that's the youth I'm fighting for. Because to shrink a little girl's childhood down to her years in elementary school, and after that, girlie, you can drown in sperm for all we care, for that men should be shot. Like Saint George on his steed is how I fight. But the uncle-daddykins hydra has so many heads, you have to spin like a windmill to defeat them, and I'm just a feeble woman, and you try taking on a serpentine dragon with a broom.

The man with a taste for juveniles, besides the perv with a head full of leaves from camping out in the bushes in front of some healthcare training institute or hotel school, where he can pop out to ask the freshly developed girls which way

it is to the post office and whether by any chance they might happen to know if it's a quarter to four yet, can also just as easily be the man sitting in his nonlivingroom on the sofa, reading the paper, watching the news on TV, and scratching his crotch, and the woman with one eye glued to him from behind her pots and pans has no idea what's swept under the rug and bubbling away inside the man's head.

You see, a TV screen isn't just a screen for the workers who operate the behemoth of television from within to project their carefully balanced selection of images and music to make us feel good, but also a screen for the man on the sofa, who effortlessly overlays the footage of parliamentary squabbles with his own fantasies, which does produce some glare, but not enough to outshine the gloss of the tight little curves and gaping slits projected in his brain, not the wilted lettuce his wife would try to serve him again that evening in a good faith effort at marital sexcapades, so that he could poke around inside it with his little knife, but a fresh head covered with a fertile layer of moist black soil, squatting on the ground, just waiting for him to pluck. And he isn't about to call his wife, granddaughter, doggie, and mouse to help him pull it out.

So far it's all just a little game, played within the safe shelter of the TV, whose eternally flickering rays act as a decoy for the outfoxed wife, so she remains dissatisfied solely with her husband's absorption in the news and too preoccupied with figuring out how to help him for any other doubts to fit in her head.

And yet they should, since as we know, her husband is an uncle-daddykins, or very well could be. Either way the point is, knocking down the wall between the kitchen and the living room won't reveal the truth, and as long as the man keeps on projecting his little daydreams onto the box's shiny glass and his heart and soul are with the girls while his ding-a-ling is up his wife's ass, we probably won't even tell the woman, it would just make her upset.

Besides, I put the phone number to their flat through the wash in my skirt pocket, and now all that's left of it, just like mine, which I didn't believe that you didn't want but it took an awful lot of convincing, is a little blue watery cloud, just a little tiny pipette's worth of ink is all that's left of the digits. But even if we could find their number in the Yellow Pages, my experience is that women who get wind of any genuine information turn into fire-breathing dragons at the slightest trifle, which suggests poor prospects for their continued partnership, so we won't be sending them any good luck wishes or tip-offs over the phone.

The reason these women are dissatisfied, I think, is because they still haven't outgrown their old-fashioned corsets, or maybe their stick-it-inner is too grand in its demands and thinks a hammer is just meant to bang all the time and isn't also designed, to some degree, for peeing, contentedly dangling down sloth-style, and just generally as a splendid decorative element, a sort of earring for the crotch, a jewel brooch, a pink

amber necklace that every now and then needs a gentle rinse of water with a drop of soothing non-sting liquid soap, and finds being inserted by and large disgusting, even if sometimes it does it as often as peeing, along with all the rest of it.

My guess is, if the woman couldn't fantasize about what a lech the man was, she wouldn't moan so happily as she loaded the plates into the dishwasher when he still wasn't home, and if he was just sitting there alone in his office until midnight, well then, the whole thing was pretty boring and nothing even to worry about, and he said he would buy her a cute little dress with the overtime he earned, which no doubt he will, but since in reality it's because the reason he stayed until midnight was he was fucking his secretary and his conscience wouldn't allow him not to make up for it, and he needs to blow off a little steam, if not for tonight, then preventatively, for nights to come, since after all, every company's got a secretary somewhere, the woman worries her pretty little head that her day might be lacking in existential depth, since all it consists of is scrubbing, vacuuming, and walking the dog. Why do that when she could be measuring moisture levels in building envelopes on a lucrative contract from the institute for monument conservation, performing an audit of the largest Czech window manufacturer, or translating a book about the history of Italian opera?

I of course realize that women today aren't just crawling around with a rag on all fours. So with all the interesting jobs they have, what would they want to go and worry their pretty

little heads for? Assuming that there was any time leftover, this could easily be the subject of another episode in my TV mystery series, since in my view women have a tendency to worry too much, and I know men have no idea why, so if anyone out there has the answer, send it my way. Could it be that that's just how their minds work and they can't be held responsible any more than the client with the deviant appetites caused by his daily sucking under the blanket when he was still a little boy? And how sad would that be, since there isn't much you can do about what mother nature endows you with.

In short, women take a lot of things too personally, but they also don't distribute their interest evenly besides. For example, they aren't nearly as concerned about protecting fourteen-year-olds from being fucked as they are about disabled girls in wheelchairs or abandoned dogs. It's also true that most fourteen-year-olds look nowhere near as heartbreaking. When I scoot down to the mall on my bike in the morning to have my espresso, I ring my bell like a madwoman and the juveniles act like they don't have ears, ignoring me and laughing their heads off the whole way to school over nothing. They don't give a shit about authority, in fact there's nothing about those budding blossoms that's heartbreaking at all, and what's more, the ones who are already prematurely getting banged like to congregate in front of establishments where a soda costs a fortune for a normal person, and the average honest working man would say to himself that the threads they have

on cost more than any decent man will ever earn in his life, and in their case he would happen to be right, though I don't know if I would call the girls dishonest. With all the hours they put in, they deserve that money. Walk out of a children's fuckshop with some cash in that cute little purse of theirs and have a little frolic.

When your work is a religious order and a racket, then your free time needs to be yay whoopee, so you can do more than just survive, because nobody wants to just listlessly cross off the days, you want to get through it in good spirits, and even hardworking young whores deserve that. Woe to those who would put them under a halogen lamp and hector them with lectures on moral decency. Those who want to sweep the swarm of bugs out from under the overturned rock, stink exposers, I guess you might call them.

Because who thinks about themselves when they're just coming up on adolescence? Bespectacled smart aleck girls and boys who have to, because you can't kill your time playing dodgeball when no one wants you on their team. I can even understand why the uncle-daddykins fancy little girls, though the cluster of retired ladies from the hallway would chase me out of the building with brooms like the devil incarnate for saying so.

I'm not the depressive type, so rather than think about the end of the world I would be more likely to imagine myself as Joan of Arc, or some persecuted witch from the fifteenth century, or the first woman in the world who learned to read, since like her I suffer from other people's dim-wittedness.

Picturing yourself as historical figures is different from tormenting yourself with visions of a secretary spreading her thighs on your husband's desk and then of the two of them doing it. Imagining those kinds of configurations, the best you can hope to do is work yourself into a lather, whereas historical personalities can serve as a model in times of difficulty. Running out of our building, say. I would run out the door and wouldn't stop till I came to the riverside, and as soon as I reached the water, despite that I'm not the depressive type, since sinking into states isn't my thing, I would burst into tears.

Apart from my molded plastic three-room suite, you see, there's no place else I could go, with my bags and the little cage with the molded-plastic yellow bird from China thrown over my shoulder, and take a rest for at least a few days.

In other words it's obvious, since I'm not lying about having a housing crisis, that I don't have too many friends, and my parents are either dead, moved away, or we have a bad relationship. For that matter, if I had grown up in a kids' home and we were to stick to the theory of the harmful effect of early experiences on development, like the boy sucking his uncle under the blanket, it might explain why I chose this profession and why I say I can understand uncle-daddykins and their desires and other perversions along those lines.

If the pensioners in our building were women of principle, though, they wouldn't give a shit about those sob stories, just like I don't give a shit about the sob stories of the men who come to my molded plastic three-room suite, and not only

because I don't have any emotional connection to them, but everyone's got a sob story and the only thing it means is they feel sorry for themselves, which might be all right, or might be perverted or a lie. When I say that I can understand uncle-daddykins, it definitely isn't a lie and it isn't perverted either. If, like me, when you shop for vegetables, you look for the youngest baby carrots and butter beans, then you can confirm there's no such thing as a carrot that's too young. Fish, yes. Not that there's anything wrong with the way the young ones taste, it's just that taking undersized fish isn't honest. When it comes to fish, people play fair, since not only can they take away your fishing license, but anyone who doesn't throw back their undersized fish is a crook, the same as the uncle-daddykins who fucks a fourteen-year-old, even if the comparison may grate on the ears, since comparing animals to people is silly. Which is why it also makes no sense to talk about the protections they have for baby lambs and goats in some countries, and how we should take a lesson from them, just as we should from the tropical islands where men undergo rites of passage into manhood, so they have fewer wimps, so that here we eat only the tough meat from grown-up animals, because killing animal young is a crime, whereas eating poor quality meat is just an annoyance, and that's called morality. That means we need to protect against a cock's natural inclination to harden at the sight of a fourteen-year-old it wants to fuck because she already has secondary sex characteristics by erecting inhibitions and laying traps of shame, or we might

wind up in a shit-covered mess, with immature women being fucked more than the fully grown, who want it more but their chassis can't take the beating it used to, though you never know, the old ones might be talked into it too, and you wouldn't have to offer twice, but we've given up on forcible regulation for that age group, so there's hardly any intercourse going on there at all anymore, and why get bogged down in someone else's concerns voluntarily, everyone's got concerns enough of their own, and to act as their personal humanitarian worker to boot? The assurance of no unwanted conception is just too small a band-aid, so the old women cluster in the hallways of old buildings and lend each other their portable blowers, since all you can buy on a pension is a piece of junk with no settings, and they fan each others' faces in the streets and help the younger women changing blouses, since they're still having hot flashes and lugging around their handbags full of spare tops like street vendors, and in fact, they could swap and sell them back and forth among themselves, why not?

Every idea over time fleshes out with details and particulars that would never have crossed your mind at first, like the one I had just now, for a pop-up market in women's blouses, where they could swap clothes and the latest news. When women get together, there's bound to be gossip, and the whole thing would organically come into being to everyone's general satisfaction, instead of it being organically commercialized and the authentic community of ladies' blouse vendors going belly up as corporations flood the market with cheap Chinese

textiles and women's handbags being even heavier than before, since low-quality Chinese textiles sweat through faster, so they would have to bring a bigger supply of blouses every day.

Do you think this bitter experience with the ruthless machinery of capitalism, which has crushed to a pulp so many people, and ideas and TV series even more flawless than mine, would make old women any softer toward the young? Given how hard their own lives are, shouldn't they have a fine-tuned sensor for the hard life in general? Horse feathers. They would rather shovel all their money and passion into sick babies and kittens than into preventing prematurely fucked-up youth.

Having compassion for those you fear doesn't happen just like that. You don't just throw the little girl some arm floaties, or pull her in nice and slow by the suit with a hook, when she's going under in a pool full of turds. Little girls are the most sensual seductresses out there, it makes old ladies break out in shivers. Why, when they need help, are they also hidden by the parliamentary coverage while the man projects them on screen in his mind? Not only that, but they can be chewing gum and frowning the whole time, while the older woman constantly has to be powdering herself with something. Then the portable blower goes and blows the powder off again, and besides, she shouldn't be frowning anyway, since not only is a woman's most beautiful jewel her smile, not fainting, and it doesn't cost a thing, but also wrinkles remain on inelastic skin, and the moment they latch on, they dig in like ticks and start to spread, like cellulite, all over your body. Then at night you

won't even want to turn on the light, and a low-cut neckline only adds to the hippo effect.

But the little girl whores don't think about any of that. They don't worry, they don't even know it exists. They don't mop anyone's floors, or calculate their taxes, and they're still more fuckable.

And these sexy little fourteen-year-old women, who can laugh in the face of not only older and elderly women, but also the ones who are just barely grown-up enough to be of legal age, and in fact they often do, these worms expect protection from the very same women who suffer as a result of their mere presence in society, because all attention is focused on them, even if the older woman is freshly blown with the blower, giving her at least a five-minute window of absolute peak chic, she's shit out of luck, and what's more, she has to act like it doesn't bother her, since she isn't five and can't engage in petty vanity, and it's about time she finally found some other interests, instead of just constantly comparing herself, grooming her appearance, and worrying her pretty little head about it over and over and over again. Still, what are you going to do, since not giving a shit may be unavoidable as a woman gets old, depending on what she eats and how well she hydrates, but not giving a shit about yourself, now that's a different story.

Maybe as part of a resolution, then all right. If worrying her pretty little head is the goal, then she could stand to suffer a tad, at least it would be more righteous. Because what says

martyrdom more than the love of a mature woman, saving fuckable babes by luring the enemy to her?

For that matter, keeping the Ten Commandments is much harder work than keeping your ass held firmly up in the air for a good ten minutes, especially when it's already a bit mushy on the sides and on the verge of shuddering from the loss of appetite, like a toddler who can't even see past the creamy lid in front of her eyes to focus on the fiftieth spoonful of pudding.

You at least, unlike the toddler, a tabula rasa, can count to yourself in your mind, recite the multiplication tables, picture animals whose names start with the letter r, but either way, you're still just waiting for the client to finish banging and get the hell out, and afterward, you can blow it all off with a sigh of relief that it was nowhere near as challenging as keeping the Ten Commandments.

Group-style

Under the kitchen sink I keep a little religious shrine. I could go on proving how traditional I am until I'm blue in the face and still most people would be opposed. It just speaks to me, intuitively. Maybe that's the object of my shrine talking.

The attitude toward religion of the women who flock in the hallway of the building where I live is at best lukewarm to tepid. Being practical women, they're thinking about the homestretch and wondering what if there really was something to it and one day Satan came and knocked on the window and said, How are your biscuits baking, wench? I'd probably drop a little shit in my drawers myself if that happened to me.

That's why I keep that little shrine beneath the sink, and it's under there because it's my own private business and not for any client snooping around my flat to find.

If it were always only one, then I could keep an eye on him, like the man on the sofa in the nonliving room from the nonkitchen, but sometimes there are three or four people in my place, even more, if I allow them to make a special arrangement.

You see, it isn't always just another woman who comes with the client. Sometimes the client himself takes it into his head to have a wild fiesta and invites over his buddies, or just some men he finds through an ad who when it rains show up in big work boots and tromp all over my entryway and then change in the same room together, like the locker room at the sports complex or pool. They're also wet like they just got out of the pool when they're in the thick of it, and it's pouring off me too, but not always, since sometimes I keep all my clothes on and just supervise, walking around and keeping a lookout.

I'm the locker room attendant, the line judge, the usher, the referee, the madame of the house, if any of them want to call me that, though my fuckshop isn't a brothel, and they're agricultural workers, service technicians, businessmen, and often they come with their ties still on, and roll them up and stuff them in their pants pockets like extralong bills.

I give them each a hanger to keep the creases out of their pants, and while I gingerly feel them out and clarify the rules, I make small talk to loosen them up, maybe ask, for example,

why pink ties with pale pig-pink shirts came to be all the rage in officewear, and if the men who are more mindful of their appearance go so far as to coordinate their outfits by wearing pink briefs and socks too, since from outside there's no way to tell.

The only way to find out is if you hit on a pink client and wait for him to undress, but I had never had the good fortune before, and no one is born knowing these things, which is why I asked, and the pink man who came with the group said that rounding out the ensemble with matching briefs and socks was actually a fine idea, and whipped out his phone and punched something in, maybe my little idea, who knows, and maybe all the pink men are out there right now walking around in rounded-out ensembles, there's no way to tell when you're on the street, and they picked it up from each other in the fitness center changing room, and that client of mine was their first prophet and I was his Mary Magdalene, taking tickets purchased at the door, the bigwigs like it theater-style, especially the little group that comes the first Thursday of every month and walks into the room next door and right away starts seething and groping and rooting their hammers around each other's holes like a little herd of pigs, while my job is to keep tabs on who does what to whom, because not everyone is allowed to do it with everyone.

But it isn't only women who fret their pretty little heads, it's the same with the client who comes in with his wife and the rest of his gang to refresh his sexual appetite, which is

notably constricted by his pink tie, though that same pink tie, the mark of a man at once both gentle and courageous, is also the reason why his belly and his hammer deserve a little fluffing up, since a man like that doesn't give up so easily, and he brings his wife with him, because they won't give up on each other and they won't give each other up either, but only up to a point, and that's why I'm there, to supervise the moves of not only the black pieces but also the white pieces who haven't found a tanning booth in their neighborhood yet, so they feel even more naked in front of the black ones than they actually are.

What makes the fretting a turn-on is that the rules forbid you from interfering in any way other than watching when your muffin's muffin does something with another muffin's muffin. In fact it's an extremely stressful turn-on, as is instantly visible from a glance at the pink tie guy's weenie. He's kept his tie on, but is otherwise totally undressed. He had the same opportunity everyone else did to roll it up and deposit it in the pocket of his pants thrown over the hanger, but it's probably a way for his wife to recognize him in case she gets too turned on and the men's faces all start to blur into one from being fucked in her Cyclops eye. It's the same thing as when her eyes sometimes go almost totally blind when she's on the crest of a sexual peak and suddenly instead it turns out to be the rolling hills of the Central Bohemian Uplands and drags the woman up and down like a tin can on a cat's tail, even if that isn't what she wanted, and the French, who know sex inside

and out, like their celebrated cheeses, call that la petite mort, the little death, and the woman looks like she may be on the verge of it right now as her sticker-inner snuggles with her husband's coworker's wife's sticker-inner, and then they're no longer snuggling but humping each other like rutting bucks that have shed their horns but are still caught up in the rush and have to get it out of their system, just like the sperm of the husband of the woman in question, whom the rules forbid from interfering or joining in with the women, and right now that torments him more than all the paperwork that awaits him tomorrow, which this wonderful party won't reduce by so much as the slightest hair, although neither will it increase it, as might be imagined by those who would like the couple to be punished in some way for this disgusting escapade, but no. That nice little stack of contracts will still be on the desk of the pink tie guy tomorrow, the same as it was today when he walked out the door at the stroke of six, only meanwhile he managed to come in the hair of the asshole husband of one of his coworkers, thinking it was that shorthaired hussy from the press section on the ground floor. It was probably all starting to blur into one for him too, even if it wasn't a rolling landscape, but just one good hill the size of Říp, assuming you count that little rotunda on top, but thank goodness even for that, since he and the wife had put more time into tandem skydiving than anything else for the past few months, and he may not have had a rotunda on the tip of his manhood, but he definitely had a drop on top there, before the spurt to

the finish, and somebody gulped it down. Maybe even that shorthaired hussy from the press section, before she vanished into the tangle of bodies, and god only knows who ended up coming into her.

If anyone knows, it ought to be, ahem, begging your pardon, me, only in general terms perhaps, but with one hundred percent certainty that the general terms are being adhered to, since that's what I'm there for, winding my way in and out, like the woman who tears the tickets, stepping over the clumps of electrified wires for the kiddie cars at an amusement park. Because not everyone is allowed with everyone else, and not only is no man allowed to join in with his wife when she's getting into it with another woman, but under the rules, actual hammering with deep penetration, obviously I'm not talking about nuzzling with the tippity tip, can take place only within the framework of married couples, period.

Otherwise the barrels of fun quickly turn into bad blood, and that's the last thing I need, if only for the sake of my furniture and glassware, which they talked me into leaving in the playroom to make it look classy, though I stacked the rest of my fragile things in a pile in the kitchen, but there's always someone who crosses the line or uses an illegal hold, some shot from out of bounds or somesuch, and a referee can't prevent these things, since he ordinarily doesn't step in until a foul occurs, what else do you expect?

Of course this makes it all sound entirely reasonable, but when your coworker's hammer is pounding your muffin's

muffin, you might call for more than a yellow card, and I had all these workplace relationships written down on paper, so when somebody stuck his fingers someplace he wasn't supposed to, then I'd give him a slap on the backside, or his honker or his hammer, and if it was the latter then he would head straight to the penalty box, meaning the couch, looking down in the dumps. Maybe because he didn't have a team to root for and his hammer hurt like a bitch from the slap I'd administered. On the other hand, he could be glad that the penalty wasn't for somebody else to take his place in his wife's sticker-inner. Occasionally the men would start calling penalties on each other and a rodeo would break out, the bigwigs having at it. While some women squeezed into the corner, so scared they practically merged into the wallpaper, others loudly chanted their boyfriend's name as he pummeled the poor little coworker the woman had been banging just a few moments before.

Afterward they always left a big stink behind, from the fuckathon, and a big pile of mud in the entryway, whenever it had poured that day or the day before and any of the big-wigs had his company car in the shop, and there was always one who did.

I would stay up wiping till after midnight, since not only do I not like waking up to a disgusting mess and having to clean it up first thing when I get back from jogging or riding my bike, but starting a new day with reminders of the night before, since I'm sure I would remember something while

mopping up their muddy bootprints, I would bet my life on it, is pointless when the night in question wasn't especially memorable, and I can easily avoid any pointless reminiscence simply by whipping my place back into shape tout de suite as soon as the door clicks shut behind the last client.

TV Episode Eight: Mind Reading and TV Episode Nine: Black Women, Thai-Koreans, and Who Knows What Else

And then the weekend is here, which my sticker-inner and I both always really look forward to, even after an evening when all I do is referee, so it isn't too much of a grind for him, and besides, my weekend is nothing so rigidly repetitious as a Saturday and Sunday off at the end of a five-day workweek, but any two days off in a row, could be Tuesday Wednesday or Sunday Monday, it all depends how the clients line up, but I declare a weekend for myself at least twice a month, whether or not there's a holiday, since the shopping mall isn't burdened by rigid hours either, so it welcomes me with open arms whenever I make my mind up to go.

Sometimes the sticker-inner and I will call it quits at sunset and start our new day on Saturday night, which means I'm the one setting out after dark to go shopping, instead of the client. One advantage to that is also that fewer people go to the mall around that time, especially if they're showing something good on TV, but usually I put off my shopping till morning too, even though, and I always tell myself I've learned my lesson for next time, then I have to deal with the crowds, even if the episode from last night wasn't that good and I'm wondering whether everyone else is thinking the same thing as me, whether we can read each other's minds, because sometimes that's how it seems. As a matter of fact, that isn't a bad idea for the final episode of my mystery series, which is going to be a cut above all those other stupid shows. Mind reading. After dealing with all the anxieties of the e-world, the handbags and the calories and the boneshakers and all the rest, it's high time for something thoughtful-minded.

My clients have even told me flat out a few times. Not only, "You read my mind," which is code for "Let's get right to it," but "You read my mind, ma'am" or "You read my mind, hon," depending whether it turns him on more for me to be a lady paid to boss him and his hammer around without his even asking for it, or if it's more of a turn-on for me to be a pussy charged to a credit card, and as soon as we shake hands I arch my back and offer up my ass and start meowing like I want him inside me this very second, and that's because the sooner I do, the sooner his rod is back to limply hanging and

141

he walks out the door, which is to say there are times when I grope around as blindly for thoughts as I do for my tampon before it sucks up too much blood and I skillfully fish it out with just two fingers, no matter how deep down it's strayed into the black hole of my Cyclops eye.

This part of the TV mystery series would have no asterisk to indicate its suitability for younger audiences, since there would be no content about the hidden mysteries of the male and female worlds, which the little ones will have plenty of time to learn later on, but the question of whether or not we can read each other's minds is actually an idea I came up with myself. I didn't just get it from my clients who use it to express their deep satisfaction with the first-class treatment provided them by me, my sticker-inner and my head, which figures out how best to tailor it to the clientele's needs within the framework of a uniquely individualized plan. But is it really me who figures it out and divines their thoughts?

For the average and above-average client, I'm a piece of ass and that's it, and they don't go that far into analyzing who it is exactly that reads their minds, but I can ask, even if they don't. Is it really me?

Or is it my sticker-inner with the tiny little head, whose brain couldn't be any bigger than a pterodactyl's, because where would it fit, in there between the villi, but he's sure thinking for himself when he starts creaming in my panties, and he doesn't need any hammer or my money-counting fingers for that.

Or maybe it is my head, as a standalone unit, since my head isn't me, just like my sticker-inner isn't, and if I'm something half and half, created from their union, then I don't know what that is, so whoever is actually reading their minds, if anyone does it intentionally, or whether that's just what they call it when someone creates that feeling of deep satisfaction in us, maybe even unintentionally, though the pleasure I bring my clients is pretty damn intentional or I wouldn't be able to talk about the hard work and strenuous effort I put into earning my daily bread, not some cinnamon raisin swirl robed in chocolate, but a coarse-grained black rye, as I hope would be clear by now.

Then again, those breads, not the fluffy whites or the ones that are sweetened, are the ones that are best for your health, and hammering is good for your health too, and to make the whole thing easier, instead of trying to track down who slept with whom and for how much, we might simply observe that it's also the best free method of acne prevention, like a woman's smile, which is free and also surely adds to one's beauty. But whereas I would bet you've never seen a whore with advanced acne, you've probably seen a tart who doesn't smile. Am I right?

When I'm in my shopping mall, I think about mind reading, though. There amid the swarm of other women, which like them I could have spared myself if I had started my weekend yesterday night instead of watching that dumb TV show. Then again, it would have had to be my idea alone, since if the other women had also wanted to spare themselves today's crush

by skipping yesterday's show, then nobody would have been spared anything. It would have been crowded yesterday night instead of this morning, that's all, in which case the notion that you should act the same way you want others to act smacks of pure humbug.

I know we already did this, but besides mind reading, the main thing I have going through my mind the whole time I'm in the mall is those women in their change of life with the handbags full of spare blouses. There might be a way to connect the two. In fact, incorporating the first episode of my series into the next-to-last one, or the other way around, sounds and looks almost as sophisticated as the décor in the boutique section, which is my favorite place to think about things. Like how many of the women around me have a supply of spare wardrobe with them at that very moment.

Because judging from their age I'd say that every other woman there carrying a bulky bag is in menopause. Or does every other woman really make such a large purchase? Or did they come to the mall already with one of those cute little blouses sticking out of the paper bag and now they're just looking for a fitting room to change in, and trying to cover it up by taking a heap of designer clothes in there with them behind the curtain, but once they change into their dry blouse from home they'll go and put them right back on the shelf?

In general, I find the idea of looking into women's bags exciting, and not just in my head, but even a little in my sticker-

inner. I can feel him coming to life right away at the thought of what nice things he might find in there, and whether it might be so lovely it surpasses even a sunset in the mountains with a view, since in that case it would be worth it to inspect everybody's bags, even if it didn't turn up till the very last bag of the last woman security escorted out the door five minutes after closing time, and I could have spared myself the whole day's inspection, but actually not, since there was no way to know in advance, and besides, all that hard work would be worth it to the sticker-inner, since anything that surpasses a sunset must be truly wonderful.

That's why I sometimes envy the men at the entrance, who can dig around inside the women's bags to their heart's content, and in fact it's even expected of them, provided they don't want to lose their job, and no one wants that, including me with my work like a loaf of black rye, so I stay looking as many years younger as possible than I am, since there's no such thing as a carrot that's too young, and it isn't against the law to look fresh and young when you're not, so there's no excuse not to. Oof, talk about hard work.

Of course the men at the door checking bags must have feet swollen as buckets from standing ten hours every day, but in exchange they have a privilege denied other mortals, unless they want a handbag to the head or, assuming he isn't a wimp, a smack in the face from the woman's male companion. Bag inspectors can rummage through any bag belonging to any woman they find attractive, or not at all and they're just curious

whether the inside of her handbag is as ugly as her face, or whether the lining is as mangy as its owner's ill-fitting pantsuit.

At any rate, that's definitely what I would be thinking, because just like dogs' appearance often resemble their owners', people's other accessories can come to look like them, so why not handbags' insides?

Of course, it goes without saying, it's mainly large purses we're talking about. Handbags and totes of various types that can hold at least a set of five tops, though preferably more, since with increasing age women are also more mindful of security, which is to say, they would rather return home in the evening with one or two blouses unused than to have too few, and it isn't just for the sense of security, because carrying more also means that they're training with heavier weight, which means a firmer figure, and even if we don't know yet whether anyone appreciates the physical fitness of menopausal women, by which I mean any dongs, hammers, or optimistic weenies, since we haven't shot that part of the first episode, women might be willing to carry even more for the sense of security it ensured if it also meant they wouldn't be caught off guard by a hammer hardening to readiness in response to their menopausal fitness, but were ready to take it on.

Still, that doesn't mean the women aren't embarrassed in front of the inspectors at the entrance to the mall. In fact that's precisely why women do it, is because of the signs of aging, and whether it's a wrinkle, thickening calves, or a suspiciously large quantity of spare blouses, isn't what matters. What matters is

the aging, and why on earth would it not be, when a woman is forty-nine, even if she says forty-eight because her birthday is the day after tomorrow, women grasp at straws like that for as long as it takes to gather up enough of them for some real visibility, even if only in the form of an oversize bag.

Another reason it struck me there might be relatively more women in menopause at the mall is because they blend in better in that environment. Even some men carry big bags there, so it almost acts to camouflage your gender, and even if not, the odds are a handbag full of blouses will go completely unnoticed amid the other bags filled with purchases of sportswear and appliances, and why shouldn't a woman suddenly be twenty-seven in that environment, since you are whatever age you feel, and you feel whatever age the men and other women allow you to be, and by the same token, what age you look is a function of what age you feel, so the women who actually are in menopause, with the shriveling sticker-inners, are the ones who look somewhere between twenty-five and thirty-five, while the ones who look menopausal are the ones who left their handbags full of tops at home or live right nearby so they didn't bother and therefore have nothing to help them blend in with the crowd of shoppers, which is a shame, because it's a pretty simple trick for making yourself look younger and I think it works, because some women, the second they walk out of the mall onto the street, this time without stopping, since the inspectors don't bother with the women who are leaving, all of a sudden look like they've aged several decades.

147

Maybe it's also the light, which is far from flattering to a woman on the street, though still not enough to explain such a dramatic transformation. Then inevitably comes the question, What next? What do they do with the clothing they bought for their twenty-seven-year-old body once they come home and realize that they're still fifty? This would account for my observation that no matter how many clothes the menopausal women buy, they still look hideous. The reason being that everything they buy they have to turn around and give away to their nieces, or ship to Africa, or package up and send to teenage girls in correctional facilities, young mothers with children, at least there's some breastfeeding there and the kids learn to speak, because either they simply can't fit in the clothes or, being older women with taste and judgement, they recognize that it just isn't the right look for their age. Of course you can also see why men would bemoan the fact that their wives shell out so much cash, since it adds nothing to their wardrobe while depleting their funds hand over fist, I mean, it's just straight-up embezzlement, really, since now there's some Somali woman wearing the money from their joint account and she can't even brag about the label on her chic designer clutch, since she doesn't know how to read.

Even with the army-level camouflage, though, I can't help it, I still feel like I can spot a handbag of menopause blouses at a hundred paces, even amid the hustle and bustle of the mall, and invariably the person holding it is a woman going

through her change of life, even if she looks under thirty and is sweet-chatting a salesman in the electronics department in the most incredibly pushy way, though you would much more likely expect her to be waiting in line for a fitting room in the women's lingerie department, checking out the teen hits, or sifting through a rack of cocktail dresses.

And that is precisely what confirms me in thinking I can read the mind of that woman, who in spite of everything is still afraid that she'll be exposed, like the emperor in new clothes, and somebody will snap at her, Get out of here, you're too old, and she'll sense that they're right, and even though she's still safely disguised, her face will suddenly sag like an overwashed tracksuit and her whole afternoon will be ruined. The fact that this young woman catches my eye and immediately sets off my menopausal handbag signal, even though she's sweet-chatting a salesman in electronics, where someone like her should have no business being, the very unlikelihood of it adds to my faith in my mind reader, purring away within the terra incognita of my body and only occasionally making itself known.

The thing is, if I were to say to myself, Ha, a menopausal handbagger, the moment I saw a woman whose appearance fit the description and who, on top of that, was lugging around a large bag, that would be just an ordinary observation, not reading minds, which is what I believe I do, and not only my clients', because what I'm telling you is I'll say it even when I see a totally young woman, and then sometimes I'll follow her out of the mall like a police officer and wait to see her

transformation when she walks out the door. But only as long as I'm not standing in line for the checkout myself or I don't have too much shopping to do, to just wander out and back in again for the sake of some woman I don't even know.

I'm really happy when my mind doesn't think too much, since not only does overthinking lead to branching off in multiple directions, which you appreciate from a plug in a flat with just one outlet, but as a human being with just one head I sure as hell don't, because after a while I can't cope, I can't keep up with it all, and the harder I try to stop it, the more it keeps running away from me, and today I'm not waiting for the second woman in front of the mall so that when she comes we can hop on my bike and my thoughts will just go away, but I can stay here as long as I want, right up until closing time, so I quick have to find some tempting cute little shop, where my thinking about the bargains to be had will crowd out all the rest I don't need.

You see, because smart alecks aren't just some people I don't like, but people who don't have it easy. Still, it's their own fault, so no tiny violins, or for me, missing that brand new chic boutique with special introductory prices on my first circuit around the mall, so that gorgeous piece didn't catch my eye till my second time around.

As soon as anyone says the words introductory prices, my sticker-inner says stop, no one's going anywhere.

I know what a cross to bear life is for my sticker-inner, which is why I put up with it when, for instance, he doesn't want to go into a clothing store offering introductory discounts because he's afraid of being introduced, and come to think of it, maybe the poor thing's afraid of having a hammer introduced because he's fed up with it and somewhat lacking in imagination in that area. Sometimes he has to be convinced even just to open up for work before an appointment with a client, but then there are times when he's just being an ordinary imp, trying to make me feel sorry for him and squeezing money out of me like a little kid because certain tampons come in a colorful box and are supposedly aerodynamic, which I wouldn't be able to tell, but probably he can, or maybe he's just got a thing for colors, since I doubt he can see the ads on TV through that little Cyclops eye of his. The outer sticker-inner likes to chime in too, usually when I try on underthings, wanting me to take out the plastic they put in the crotch of panties and bikini bottoms to keep customers from soiling them.

When it comes to that I put my foot down, but it's exhausting to debate about it, and then I'm in the fitting room for half an hour and the other customers grumble, thinking I must be trying on the whole year's collection, even though I've been standing behind the curtain the entire time in a single pair of panties, insisting that we have to leave the plastic in, while the outer sticker-inner just keeps on saying no.

Luckily, women's lingerie and toiletries are the only areas where my stick-it-inner and outer stick-it-inner force their

opinion, they couldn't care less as far as the rest of my wardrobe's concerned, and even if I walked around looking like a total bum, they wouldn't say a peep.

Because it's true what I said earlier, that my stick-it-inner is a model of material restraint, whereas when it comes to the seasonal hits — spring, summer, fall, winter — I often fall for them, even though it's usually just junk they're trying to get rid of, but he just lets all that go right by, watching with a patronizing smile spread across the straight line that he settles into when he's relaxed.

He can afford to laugh too, the smart aleck. Even if he was the extravagant type, that black hole of his isn't designed for anything but stuffing up inside, no external dressing up like the Baku-Ceyhan pipeline or any of those other tubes running through Central Asia, not even for a short distance, there just isn't anything there to put clothes on.

So that beautiful piece that caught my eye on my second go-round of the shopping mall was a gorgeous, deep salmon-colored cashmere scarf, the kind of piece that's opulent yet at the same time restrained, which you buy because you have refined taste, and also the money, but mainly the taste, since people with refined taste also tend to be wealthy, since otherwise no one would ever know about their refined taste. It's all extremely sophisticated and very convenient for flirting with wealthy men, since not only poor women want rich men, but rich women too, but rich men prefer rich women, or at

any rate they prefer them to a poor woman who doesn't have anything to make her shine and besides that is broke.

We could make a TV mystery out of it, why is it this way, not some other, and how everybody loves money, but it reminds me of those programs they make about threshing hay. I'm not sure if money holds the same attraction for everyone, and besides, I'm sure there are people for whom money is meaningless, just like there are those truly principled shrinking violets who, despite getting me paid for in advance, turn around at the door, and men who, if they wanted, could have me fulfill their every desire, yet just up and leave without getting off, so not everybody loves money, even if most won't turn up their nose at it.

Also, just as many shrinking violets are nothing but homebodies who treat me like I'm roast pigeon, just stabbing their hammers into my behind, and most of the ones who turn up their noses at money just don't know how to make enough of it to truly enjoy it. When money's just for paying utilities, school lunches, and milk and bread and milk and bread, it really is more a worry than a joy, and if I were in their shoes, I would probably rather have it all withdrawn from circulation too, but I've got a little fistful of cash to throw around, for that salmon-colored cashmere scarf, say, even if it's not as though my neck would be cold without it, and that's my idea of surplus, which is why when I go shopping it's nothing but a sheer delight.

Which is to say I take a nice long look at that scarf, all nicely arranged on that nice mannekin there in the shopping

mall, and I'm aware of every hitch. Not only does it carry a substantial little price tag, but the mannekin it's hanging on is also really fancy, and so is all the rest of what the mannekin's wearing besides the scarf, and sometimes people just want to look like her and forget that they're only buying the scarf, and then when they get home in front of the mirror and wrap it around their neck like a Priessnitz compress and see how it looks with their worn-out overcoat, they're inevitably disappointed. It's the same with the shampoo and the instant spaghetti bolognese in a bag. When you wash your hair, you don't look anything like the lovely lady in the commercial, and when you make the spaghetti, all you have in common with the pretty little tight-assed homemaker on TV, who goes straight to seventh heaven when she makes the spaghetti, and with the family tranquillity she and her husband and two lovely children enjoy as they stand over the steaming pot, the only thing in common between their TV commercial home and your real one is the round kitchen-slash-livingroom table, and not only that, but to top it all off, yours has a wobbly leg. Which is to say, I think all these things through so I won't fall for them, and I think them through so hard even the women in menopause passing by in young person's camouflage, with their handbags full of spare blouses, can't disturb me when I'm in the thick of it.

Ultimately, I walk away with one thing or another, a pair of patent leather shoes, even though, yet again, they didn't have them in turkey-head red polished to the sheen of a whip,

a salmon-colored scarf, and a few household items to keep the fuckshop from feeling slighted and so I could practice my altruism, like some new table settings and sheets for the bed. I buy sheets more often than anything else, due to the high turnover rate, with the nicest ones reserved for work, and the older ones, once they're retired, I use for nights with little old me, which I set aside for myself like an overbooked celebrity, along with weekends, whenever a window opens up, because on nights when it's a clear dark sky with stars, my three-room suite tends to be all full up and I don't lie down till dawn, and sometimes not even then, if the client pays for full service plus sleepover, but they snore or don't smell good, so as soon as they fall asleep, I turn on the TV and flip through the channels or iron clothes till morning, since any other household work might disturb them. They all do it occasionally. The violent ones, the whinikers, the uncle-daddykins — sometimes for them I have to play a little girl, but there are also the ones who undress me and then, instead of wham bam thank you ma'am, I sit and wait half an hour, only to find them wiped out, snoring away in the bathtub with my panties on their head, either that or I accidentally confide in them about my shrine while making small talk and then they insist on doing it there, in front of the kitchen cabinet underneath the sink, or they don't want me to strip and instead they just take a pair of scissors and cut a little fuckhole for their hammer in my stockings, and then afterwards of course I charge them extra for that, like a special edition.

Then again, some show up swinging a plastic bag in their hand, and I know what I'm in for then, because the plastic baggers love fairy-tale characters and can only get off in costume, which they carry in a special suitcase, separate from their other things. There tend to be no problems with them, and it could be a laugh doing it with the evil wizard, Pinocchio, or Rumplestiltskin if it wasn't my job, and those getups of theirs are so lame even a dog wouldn't piss on them. Then there are the ones who want to play animals, or animals with a story, so we'll spend an hour being camels crossing the desert to an oasis, who slake their thirst by having sex multiple times, or a lion and lioness, where the lion mounts me from behind with his teeth sunk into my neck the whole time, it's pretty unoriginal, not to mention uncomfortable.

I don't know why, but the ones who like to play animals are always set on doing it multiple times. They probably think of nature as this wild place, with all the animals running around screwing their heads off, when actually, except for a few weeks of rutting each year, they hardly ever screw at all, and if some lioness came along and started slurping some lion's dipstick since she had nothing better to do and it was out of season, he'd probably give her a proper licking, and I don't mean with his tongue. All those tiger-and-deer or cat-and-mouse games fall under the category of violent play, like in kindergarten, when they play donkey and make the class punching bag carry them all around on his back, only it doesn't have any effect yet on the little knob between his legs.

For my cat character, one client even brought whiskers for me to stick to my face, I hope they weren't plucked from some woman's outer sticker-inner, with special cases you never know, and a spiked collar, which I was supposed to use to pin him up against the wall, like a cat does to a mouse when it's just about to kill it, and being on the edge like that would bring him to a boil. The spikes probably hurt a little, but no more than taking a lash to someone's ass, and that's common practice for me.

In general, stories are popular. There was a hilarious thing with one of my regular clients who always wanted to act out the same story that had been on the porn channel a few days before, right down to the last detail, including the names, Claudia and Günther, Gisele and Klaus, Elfriede and Johannes, so that's who we were, once a week for a full thirty minutes, the same length as on TV too, so we wouldn't have to leave anything out, or improvise anything on the spot to fill the extra time. At first I wondered where he came up with all those ideas, but then one day I figured it out, and the next time I was ready for him, props and everything. The first episode wasn't even that hard, fucking a hot young cleaning girl in the darkened hallway of an elementary school after parent-teacher confer-ences, which is actually a fairly plausible scenario, at least as far as these types of fantasies go. I've got a whole closet full of buckets and rags and cleaning products and mops, and we ended up doing the scene in there too, and my client, bless his heart, was tremendously pleased, not to mention surprised

that I knew how it all went, which definitely also helped. As a matter of fact, he was one of the ones who said I read his mind, but unless he was a complete moron, it surely must have dawned on him that we had just watched the same porn.

I would almost even bet that he thought about me later on, when he watched the next installment, probably soaped his shaft up nice and good, why wouldn't he, and while he was watching too, I'm sure of it, and even after he stopped coming round the fuckshop. And there were plenty more like him. One of the most popular routines, for instance, was pretend rape during housework. One client even brought a washboard with him and hammered me over the edge of the bathtub, not the sink, he said, the angle wasn't sharp enough, I needed to be bent over more, so he hammered me on the tub while I washed my laundry, which, as it happened, I needed to do anyway. Others liked the backdrop of a roaring vacuum cleaner, or for me to be brushing my teeth, or kneading dough in a bowl, dressed in a kitchen apron with flour all over me, so they could tiptoe up to me from behind and take me with my clothes on, just my panties around my ankles.

For some men, it just doesn't work without those nice little props, and maybe some of them were just bullshitting to try to seem more interesting, but there are men out there who really can't get it up without a clothesline or leather gloves or hair rollers or tutus or a toothbrush, and so we would prod and tease their hammer with those lovely little tools until finally she was convinced, and ninety-nine times out of a hundred,

she would graciously admit defeat and submit, like a good little lady, until finally she exploded into me, on me, or on whatever costume I happened to be wearing that day.

As far as taking it to go, back to the car they had come in, say, or out to some underpass, or a dirt road outside of town, or in the bushes, or the locker room at a public pool, or, and this I found particularly disagreeable, a fitting room in the women's lingerie department at my favorite mall, where I go regularly, at least once a month, absolutely not. It's either my place or nowhere, although if we did do it in a fitting room in my favorite department, which wouldn't work, since they know me too well and I would never be able to show my face in there again after that, at least it would teach my outer sticker-inner a lesson for making such a fuss over that teeny bit of plastic when I was trying on panties, so that's what you get, there are far worse things that could happen to you, now hold that client nice and tight, I think he would probably be pretty teed off at me. But that's how it goes, I've got rules, and once I back down on them, life turns into a can of worms, the same way it does when you let people fuck little girls, even if they're well developed. Even if they nonchalantly chew gum while it's happening, as if they didn't give a fig, even if the considerable extra earnings will certainly help them improve their wardrobe, and even if some smart ass who caught the drip from girls in Bangladesh points out that there are trop- ical islands where girls get married at twelve and a half, and the whole village gathers in a circle around the newlyweds

to clap and chant in time with the thrusts of the groom as he consummates the marriage.

It's hard to defend values when people in different places value things differently, and why not take inspiration from elsewhere when we live in an e-world where we can share whatever we want, and I myself wear a scarf made of cashmere from some highland sheep and it doesn't strike me as strange at all, so why not nail a twelve-year-old?

The reason I'm traditional is that's just the way my molecules are arranged, that's how my mummykins and dadsy made me, and I don't intend to change, and the only ones harmed are the wives, and they're adults and I don't know them, and it wasn't my idea to tan their hubbies' hides.

People want everything so neatly arranged. The lovely young bride from Bangladesh, drugs like the Dutch, food like the French, and sweep the rest of life into the closet with the clutter that gets in your way, the way almost every civilized country in the world has done so far. But the fact that in Bangladesh you can have your foot cut off for fucking another man's wife or stealing your neighbor's cobra, in Holland your kids sit in a classroom full of dirty Arabs who spend their recess murmuring prayers, and in France you can't stuff your face just with camembert and champagne, the truffles and frogs come with it, that's the part of the puzzle that everyone wants to leave out, just like I want to cut that one damn episode of my mystery series.

I'm not saying we shouldn't learn from other countries. I would support having manhood tests, and even that ban

on eating animal young makes sense, I'll admit, though a tenderloin of veal doesn't upset me nearly as much as a sickly man, but all this e-griping by everyone is getting rather tiring.

With me everyone gets his thirty minutes, or sixty, or ninety, or, if need be, one hundred and twenty. Those are the only options available on my menu, and I don't see why other things in the world can't also be more cut-and-dried. Why is it that every small corner shop carries five kinds of tomato paste, and even I myself, in the course of plying my traditional trade, can be classified as an entrepreneur, a professional woman of ill repute, a courtesan, a businesswoman, a tart, a psychologist, and a fuckclub operator. I would love to have a pigeonhole and not have to swim through the cluster of old ladies in the hallway of our building like a dolphin, so instead I could ask them about their illnesses and tell them truthfully that my day was pretty worthwhile, it was certainly worth the cash I earned.

Not everything's possible, true. Even my clients walk away less than satisfied from time to time, and I say it with a slight blush, though it's nothing to be ashamed of, since nowadays you can get anything you want redone, your tits, your sticker-inner, not to mention your nose, your chin, and practically everything else, except for one thing, which is also related to coming from somewhere else, and to the desire to be inspired, which I also support, with a few qualifications, but whatever new skin I pay for, it isn't going to be yellow or black, which, according to some of my clients, is the guaranteed fastest way to make money these days. Rubbing coal all over myself before

a trick isn't going to do it. My proportions, which are equally as important as color, if not more, would still be the same, plus the client would end up looking like a miner coming up from the pit, which as a profession nowadays is relatively passé.

When a client insists, I give him the number for the Sultry Jungle service, and every now and then they also send someone my way. Someone who's had his fill of chocolate skin and slant-eyed toothpicks with no ass to grab and has figured out that this is where his roots are: east, west, home is best, and that old Czech ass beats all the rest. The type who just needs to try some things out before clambering and slogging his way to the glorious truth, and after all why not, we're all trying to find ourselves in one way or another. My fuckshop also isn't the business I lost my virginity to. It took a while for me to wise up. I just don't get what it is about black women and Thai-Koreans and I don't what else, I can't really tell all those Asians apart, so I don't see what makes them so superb that men specifically ask for them, and if I were to hold a popular vote right now on whether or not this should be part of our TV mystery series, I think I could count on a forest of hands and cries of Hear, hear, because it's a subject that, number one, is highly relevant in our e-society of mixing and diversity, number two, it relates to minorities, and anything related to them is good, number three, exposing the truth is good, number four, learning about ourselves is good, number five, learning about other nations, ethnicities and races is good, plus also relevant, the same as with minorities and mixing, and number

six, exploring human sexuality in a new and different way is also good, and the management plan is ready and I boldly say with near certainty OK'd, seeing as it's very timely and isn't afraid to get to the crux of the matter, and it's bound to be a hit with viewers, since they'll be able to tell right away which character's which based on their color, so they won't have to keep any names in their head, which I must say I can't stand when I'm watching TV — having to remember names to understand what's going on, since I often care about that, but hardly ever about the names, and foreign ones you can't even pronounce, they're the absolute worst, and some of the workers at Sultry Jungle have names like that, but thanks to their helpful spectrum of colors the audience won't have to bother with them. I doubt anyone here still owns a black-and-white TV. This isn't some village in Romania, right?

I hope the girls from Sultry Jungle really get into the shoot and throw themselves into it with the same enthusiasm as they bring to hunting wolves. From what my clients tell me… I almost got a little bit jealous of their skills.

In the Tanning Bed?

I still have a few weak points in my game. For instance, I can't keep up fellatio for an hour and a half, oh well. There's always something new to learn. I don't let my shortcomings get me down. Especially since I know from my previous businesses that once you achieve full mastery of a job's requirements, to the point where there are no more struggles with misunderstandings or technical operations, then sooner or later Mrs. Boredom comes rushing in in her poulaines, and apart from the money, what keeps me hanging on in this work is the diversity of clients I get to hang on to and the opportunity for continuous professional growth. I can always be better, even

if, in light of my age, I probably can't raise my rates. Then again, no amount of professionalism by the women at Sultry Jungle will give them lovely peachy skin either, which may be unfair, but we already covered the topic of old age and injustice previously, and the questions we raised were a) whether anyone would appreciate women in menopause and would appreciate sticking it into their physically fit bodies, hardened by the carrying around of heavy handbags, and b) why women constantly worry their little heads when they have such intriguing employment. In fact, we included this topic already in two of the series' episodes, so it's been addressed. And even if not, I still have the feeling I'm constantly repeating myself.

In short, whether I can look forward to an increase in pay or a decrease, I can certainly grow my professionalism, and growth, after all, is the main goal for a professional woman like me. Although I wonder.

I wonder why I so quickly lost confidence and now, all of a sudden, I'm at a total loss. Probably due to an excess in sincerity on my part, and a failure to think about the homestretch the way the retired women in my building do, who at least keep their religion at a lukewarm ninety-eight point six, in case the holy ding-dang-dong were to show up out of the blue and ask, So what've you been up to all these years? At least that will keep them from going straight up the chimney. As for me, not only don't I keep my religion at body temperature, but the cold from the draft in my little shrine beneath the sink can get pretty bad, which happens whenever the good-looking

muscle men outside, where that fat ugly girl sits who uses too much soap and probably nobody loves, are doing something with the pipes and they turn off the hot water, so an icy draft comes off the pipe that drains the sink. Then my hands get all red from doing the dishes, and sometimes even rubbing them with Nivea creme doesn't help. But I can't moisturize my shrine, since what would I tell the little angel if he actually did fly in one day and say, What have you been up to? You know, I've got my eye on you, and I can lower my eyes and bat my eyelashes for my clients, but the angel hasn't paid up front and he doesn't have anything down there to grow and get hard anyway, or does he?

So better moisturize me. Not my sticker-inner as usual, but my whole body, all over, to make sure I'll last for you another couple paydays. Rub it all over my splendid alabaster body, like the Lenin mausoleum, since I'm just a little knot of flesh too, like all the other big mistakes, and what exactly I did wrong I would really like to know, but I guess that no longer matters now.

Now my body is prepared for the last rites, extreme unction. Laid out in a long stroller for adults that runs on a timer, controlled by some e-device glowing red, with them watching me through a camera to make sure my heart keeps going tick-tock-tick. I'm right here, waiting to see if that little angel will come. Because some things just take time. For now it's just a test, and I'll close my eyes now, but you know this whole thing's just a game and there's nothing at all to worry about.

Translator's Note

In writing this book, the author herself has publicly said that she was strongly influenced by Elfriede Jelinek. Barbora Schnelle, a feminist theater scholar who has translated several of Jelinek's works into Czech, told *FEMA* magazine in 2012, "When I discovered Jelinek in the early '90s, it was something totally new. I had never seen a literary work that worked the language so thoroughly. In Jelinek, you can see how language is like a sponge soaked with meanings, about which we often haven't the slightest clue until we start to squeeze it and the issues come pouring out, drop by drop, whole floods of topics hidden beneath the guise of innocent-sounding words. But

now we also have women writers here in our own country who can pare words down to the bone, turning idioms inside out to expose undreamed of connections, digging into language and the world it creates in a critical way. Mainly, I have in mind Petra Hůlová and her novel *Three Plastic Rooms*. To me, it's one of the most innovative books in contemporary Czech literature."

There's no such thing as an easy translation. Every language presents its own unique challenges. In general, Czech is trickier to bring into English than, say, Spanish or French, but more straightforward than, for example, Chinese or Arabic. To some readers this will be obvious, but the reason why I say "in general" is that the difficulty of any particular translation depends as much on what a writer chooses to do with their language as it does on the inherent features of the language itself.

As Barbora Schnelle says in the quote above, in this novel—*Umělohmotný třípokoj*, translated here as *Three Plastic Rooms*—Petra Hůlová chose to do several unusual things with Czech that required special consideration to bring into English. These innovations, along with the subject matter, are what set the book apart from so many of its peers, so I felt they were worthy of comment.

To start with the biggest and most obvious: The narrator of this novel uses an impressive array of terms to refer to sex organs. But every single review I read of this book in the Czech press called attention to the two she uses most frequently:

rašple (for "penis") and *zandavák* (for "vagina"). Both of these are invented, in the sense that they haven't been used before to refer to genitalia, but whereas *rašple* is a preexisting word repurposed—a noun meaning "rasp," or "file"—*zandavák* is a noun wholly of the author's invention, derived from the transitive verb *zandávat* (alternative spelling, *zandavat*), meaning "to insert," "to put into," "to plug." The authoritative *Slovník spisovného jazyka českého* (Dictionary of Standard Czech) offers the following usage examples: *z. do kapsy zápisník* ("put a notebook in the pocket"), *zandávat do láhve zátku* ("insert a cork in the bottle"), *z. si uši* ("plug one's ears," using the reflexive pronoun *si*). It also gives examples in which the meaning differs: *kalamář, jenž se opatrně zandavá* ("the ink, which is carefully applied"), *zandavat dvířka* ("close the [oven] door"), and *lidem ústa zandávat* ("shut people's mouths"). Not to get bogged down in grammar, but there also exists another form of the verb, *zandat*, which the SSJČ defines as 1. "to put something into something [else] so that it is inside, so that it is hidden"; 2. "to close or seal something off by insertion"; 3. "to cover." Additionally, in modern-day gadgetry parlance, *zandávat* is often used to mean the opposite of *vyndávat*—"insert" vs. "remove"—in connection with batteries, USB cords, and SIM cards. One final consideration is the suffix *-ák* in *zandavák*. Although it can signify many things, one of its most frequent uses is to signify a tool. Over the months I worked on *Three Plastic Rooms*, I went through several different translations of the term (including "plug-in," "inputter," and "tuckaway") until

one day a Czech friend described it to me as a word she might use to ask someone to hand her a kitchen utensil whose real name she didn't know: *Podej mi ten zandavák*—and suddenly what came to mind was "Hand me that sticker-inner thingy."

In addition to *zandavák*, Hůlová also uses several variations on it—*zandávadlo*, *zandavátko*, and *zandaváček* (a diminutive of *zandavák*)—as well as the modification *předzandávadlí*. For the first three, in some instances I used "stick-it-inner" instead of "sticker-inner"—not slavishly, every single time, but where to me it felt right and made sense. As for the last, the prefix *před-* would typically indicate "pre-" or "fore-" in anatomical terms, but in the novel it clearly suggests the outer part of the female genitalia, and since I couldn't come up with a translation that made sense using those prefixes, in English *předzandávadlí* became the "outer sticker-inner" (and, in one case, the "outer stick-it-inner"). There is also a single occurrence of the variant *nandavátko*—from the verb *nandávat/nandat*, meaning "to add (on top of)," "to load up," "to heap on," though it can also mean "to apply" (*nandavátko* is the Czech term for a lip gloss applicator). In the end, though, as always, the translation has to make sense in context, rather than just adhering to what the dictionary says, so I translated it as "slipper-inner."

The narrator of *Three Plastic Rooms* uses many words for a man's erectile organ over the course of the book, but her favorite one is *rašple*. Both standard English translations ("rasp" and "file," as noted above) I ruled out almost right from the start, because of their multiple, potentially distracting conno-

tations—I didn't want readers thinking of the sound a person makes when they have a sore throat, or of something you use to hold papers, or of an object on a computer, especially since the Czech word is unambiguous. The fact that the verb forms *rašplit/rašplovat* ("to file" or "to rasp") and *rašplení* ("filing" or "rasping") appear in the text as many times as they do settled the matter even more solidly; again, clarity was my priority. The question, however, was what to use instead? The answer came as a result of the verb the narrator uses most for the act of sexual intercourse: *hoblovat* (and variants). This is a woodworking term, meaning "to plane," but is also common Czech slang for sex—in other words, not a Hůlová invention. So, after considering all the tools that might conceivably also mean "penis" and the verbs that go with them (I also toyed with "chisel" for a while), ultimately I decided to translate *rašple* as "hammer," putting at my disposal even more variations in verb than the Czech narrator has with *rašplení* and *hoblování*: hammering, banging, pounding, nailing. A trade-off, to be sure, but the gain in verbs seemed more than worth the loss of noun.

A final note on genitalia: Another innovation of Hůlová's that every Czech review of the novel commented on was the gender reversal at play in *zandavák* and *rašple*. Czech has three grammatical genders—masculine, feminine, neuter—with the word "penis" gendered masculine and "vagina" feminine. But in *Three Plastic Rooms*, the noun the narrator usually uses for "penis," *rašple*, is feminine, whereas the noun she favors for "vagina," *zandavák*, is masculine. This creates a comedic effect

that English offers no way to reproduce that I could think of, except to refer to the hammer as "she" and the sticker-inner as "he." Still, even here Hůlová—or her narrator—plays with expectations, employing variant forms of both nouns that are sometimes of a different gender: For the masculine *zandavák*, in addition to *zandaváček* (the masculine diminutive of *zandavák*), she also uses *zandávadlo* and *zandavátko*, both neuter; and for *rašple*, she also uses *rašplička* (feminine diminutive), *rašplidlo* (neuter), *rašplík* (masculine), and *rašplíček* (masculine diminutive of *rašplík*). I don't want to bore readers by listing here all the different ways I translated these words, especially since they don't appear that many times. The point is to know that Hůlová is working the language in these ways and that my translation had to reckon with this.

The last stylistic feature I will mention is the narrator's extensive use of diminutives. Czech, like other Slavic languages, is very rich in diminutive forms, used to express smallness, affection, familiarity, or some combination of these. In *Three Plastic Rooms*, Hůlová creates new diminutive nouns and diminutive verbs alike. To some extent, I dealt with this simply by adding the word "little," a rote solution, though often adequate; at other times I used the suffix "-kins," or added the adjective pair "tender young," for a childish yet simultaneously creepy effect, which I felt was the main impact of the diminutives in the Czech, particularly in the most disturbing scenes concerning sex.

* * *

In closing, I'd like to acknowledge and thank my Czech informants here in New York, Ivana Husáková and Irena Kovářová, both of whom I consulted with on this translation, as well as Petra herself, who not only fielded extensive questions from me, but has warmly hosted me in her home on my past several visits to Prague. I am grateful to count her as a friend.

Alex Zucker
Brooklyn, NY
September 2017

Also available from Jantar Publishing

FOX SEASON AND OTHER SHORT STORIES
by Agnieszka Dale

Agnieszka Dale's characters all want to find greatness, but they realise greatness isn't their thing. But what is? And what is great anyway? In *Peek-a-boo*, a mother breastfeeds her child via Skype, at work. In *Hello Poland*, a man reunites with his daughter in a world where democracy has been replaced by user testing. In other short stories, people bow and are bowed to. They feed foxes or go fishing. They kiss the fingers of those they love while counting to ten.

CHILDREN OF OUR AGE
by A.M. Bakalar

Karol and his wife are the rising stars of the Polish community in London but Karol is a ruthless entrepreneur whose fortune is built on the backs of his fellow countrymen. The Kulesza brothers, mentally unstable Igor and his violent brother Damian, dream about returning to Poland one day. A loving couple, Mateusz and Angelika, believe against all odds that good things will happen to people like them. Gradually, all of these lives become dramatically entwined, and each of them will have to decide how far they are willing to go in pursuit of their dreams.

www.jantarpublishing.com

Also available from Jantar Publishing

IN THE NAME OF THE FATHER AND
OTHER STORIES
by Balla

Translated from the Slovak by Julia & Peter Sherwood

Balla is often described as 'the Slovak Kafka' for his depictions
of the absurd and the mundane. *In the Name of the Father*
features a nameless narrator reflecting on his life, looking
for someone else to blame for his failed relationship with
his parents and two sons, his serial adultery, the breakup
of his marriage and his wife's descent into madness.

BURYING THE SEASON
by Antonín Bajaja

Translated from the Czech by David Short

An affectionate, multi-layered account of small town life in central
Europe beginning in the early 1930s and ending in the 21st Century.
Adapting scenes from Fellini's *Amarcord*, Bajaja's meandering
narrative weaves humour, tragedy and historical events into a series
of compelling nostalgic anecdotes.

www.jantarpublishing.com

Also available from Jantar Publishing

BLISS WAS IT IN BOHEMIA
by Michal Viewegh

Translated from the Czech by David Short

A wildly comic story about the fate of a Czech family from
the 1960s onwards. At turns humorous, ironic and sentimental,
an engaging portrait of their attempts to flee from history
(meaning the 1968 Soviet invasion of Czechoslovakia) – or
at least to ignore it as long as possible… Light-hearted and
sophisticated at once, this is a book that reminds us that
comedy can tackle large historical subjects successfully.

GRAVELARKS
by Jan Křesadlo

Translated from the Czech by Václav Z J Pinkava

Zderad, a noble misfit, investigates a powerful party figure
in 1950s Czechoslovakia. His struggle against blackmail,
starvation and betrayal leaves him determined to succeed
where others have failed and died. Set in Stalinist era Central
Europe, *GraveLarks* is a triumphant intellectual thriller
navigating the fragile ambiguity between sado-masochism,
black humour, political satire, murder and hope.

www.jantarpublishing.com

Also available from Jantar Publishing

A KINGDOM OF SOULS
by Daniela Hodrová

Translated from the Czech by Véronique Firkusny and Elena Sokol

Through playful poetic prose, imaginatively blending historical and cultural motifs with autobiographical moments, Daniela Hodrová shares her unique perception of Prague. *A Kingdom of Souls* is the first volume of this author's literary journey — an unusual quest for self, for one's place in life and in the world, a world that for Hodrová is embodied in Prague.

PRAGUE. I SEE A CITY...
by Daniela Hodrová

Translated from the Czech by David Short

Originally commissioned for a French series of alternative guidebooks, Hodrová's novel is a conscious addition to the tradition of Prague literary texts by, for example, Karel Hynek Mácha, Jakub Arbes, Gustav Meyrink and Franz Kafka, who present the city as a hostile living creature or labyrinthine place of magic and mystery in which the individual human being may easily get lost.

www.jantarpublishing.com